W9-AUD-057

"Don't you think it's just *a little dangerous* to ask a perfect stranger to have sex with you?"

Lucy's mouth fell open. Nick shifted uncomfortably in his chair and wondered if he might have possibly misunderstood her. Possibly made an asinine fool of himself. And just possibly turned this into the worst Monday on record.

"You think I want you to...?" She moistened her lips with her tongue. "To *pay* you to..."

"I don't want you to get the wrong impression," he stammered. "It's not that you're not appealing. I think you're absolutely gorgeous."

Lucy narrowed her eyes in disbelief.

"All right, maybe not gorgeous. I mean...it's been a long time for me, so any woman looks pretty good...."

She raised one golden eyebrow, daring him to bury himself even deeper.

Unfortunately, Nick could never refuse a dare. "You're very appealing for a librarian. I'm sure if the circumstances were different..."

Lucy crossed her arms over her chest. "The circumstances will never be different, Mr. Chamberlin. Your virtue is safe with me."

Dear Reader,

Many of you have been watching and enjoying the Harlequin movies. The December movie, *Recipe for Revenge,* is based on a Love & Laughter novel, *Bullets Over Boise,* by one of our "finds" (i.e. a first-time author). Moreover, the author, Kristin Gabriel, has another hilarious, romantic story on sale now called *Monday Man.* What happens when a mild-mannered librarian meets a tough ex-con? He's knocked to his knees, of course! I hope you enjoy *Monday Man,* and in December don't forget to tune in to *Recipe for Revenge*!

Jenna McKnight spins a delightful tale of a hero who seems lost in time and a heroine who doesn't believe in heroes. Place this complication in a drafty English castle, add a slightly kooky grandfather and one precious daughter, stir in a dash of mischief and you have *The Wedding Knight!* If you like knights in shining armor, you'll love this book.

Enjoy some love and laughter,

Malle Vallik

Malle Vallik
Associate Senior Editor

MONDAY MAN

Kristin Gabriel

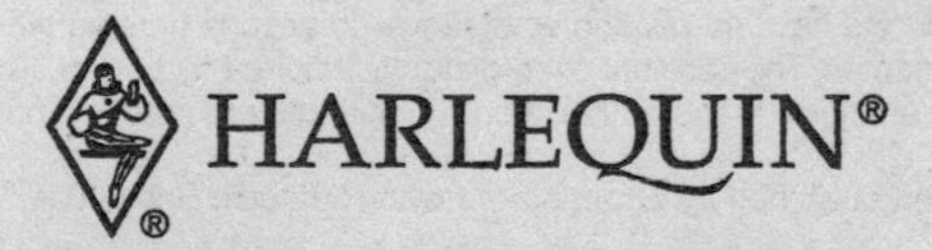

TORONTO • NEW YORK • LONDON
AMSTERDAM • PARIS • SYDNEY • HAMBURG
STOCKHOLM • ATHENS • TOKYO • MILAN • MADRID
PRAGUE • WARSAW • BUDAPEST • AUCKLAND

If you purchased this book without a cover you should be aware that this book is stolen property. It was reported as "unsold and destroyed" to the publisher, and neither the author nor the publisher has received any payment for this "stripped book."

ISBN 0-373-44056-1

MONDAY MAN

Copyright © 1998 by Kristin Eckhardt

All rights reserved. Except for use in any review, the reproduction or utilization of this work in whole or in part in any form by any electronic, mechanical or other means, now known or hereafter invented, including xerography, photocopying and recording, or in any information storage or retrieval system, is forbidden without the written permission of the publisher, Harlequin Enterprises Limited, 225 Duncan Mill Road, Don Mills, Ontario, Canada M3B 3K9.

All characters in this book have no existence outside the imagination of the author and have no relation whatsoever to anyone bearing the same name or names. They are not even distantly inspired by any individual known or unknown to the author, and all incidents are pure invention.

This edition published by arrangement with Harlequin Books S.A.

® and TM are trademarks of the publisher. Trademarks indicated with ® are registered in the United States Patent and Trademark Office, the Canadian Trade Marks Office and in other countries.

Printed in U.S.A.

A funny thing happened...

There's nothing I like better than curling up with a good book. As a teenager, I got my dream job working at a local library. Surrounded by a veritable buffet of books, I spent the majority of my workday reading between the shelves! That experience led me to create Lucy, a librarian with a love of books and a yearning for adventure. But she'll find more trouble than the heroines in her favorite novels before her story is through. So grab a cup of hot chocolate, curl up in your favorite corner and enjoy *Monday Man*.

—Kristin Gabriel

Books by Kristin Gabriel

HARLEQUIN LOVE & LAUGHTER
40—BULLETS OVER BOISE

Don't miss any of our special offers. Write to us at the following address for information on our newest releases.

Harlequin Reader Service
U.S.: 3010 Walden Ave., P.O. Box 1325, Buffalo, NY 14269
Canadian: P.O. Box 609, Fort Erie, Ont. L2A 5X3

For my sister, Linda,
who can always make me laugh.

1

MONDAYS WERE BAD DAYS for Nick Chamberlin. He'd come down with the chicken pox on a Monday. He'd wrecked his '79 Thunderbird on a Monday. He'd kissed his first girl on a Monday. Okay, technically that was a good thing. Only, the girl of his seven-year-old dreams didn't appreciate his advances and promptly knocked out his front tooth, which was eventually repaired by a sadistic dentist. On a Monday.

But that was all a very long time ago. Surely, today would be different. He was older now. Wiser. Immune to chicken pox and fast cars and dangerous women.

Nick studied the guy seated across the booth from him. A small ink stain bled though the pocket of his crisp white shirt, and a spot of ketchup smeared the front of his green clip-on tie. His plastic name tag read Captain Robby and his freckles and peach fuzz told Nick the kid couldn't be a day over seventeen.

A Monday-killer if he ever saw one.

''Interesting résumé, Mr. Chamberlin,'' Robby said, flipping the pages in the blue-bound folder. ''We've never had a cop apply at Farley's Fish Hut before.''

''*Ex*-cop,'' Nick clipped.

Robby nodded. ''Right.'' Then he folded his freckled hands together and cleared his throat. ''One of my duties here is to hire responsible, dedicated people to serve on our crew. You'll have to start out as a cabin boy even though you're—'' Robby flipped over the employment application ''—thirty-three years old. That means you're not allowed to run the cash register or operate the French fry machine. But with some self-motivation and hard work you can advance to deckhand, then first mate, and maybe after that...'' his reedy voice grew cocky ''...even a captain.''

Nick closed his eyes and reminded himself he didn't have any other viable options. ''When can I start?''

When Robby didn't answer, he opened his eyes and found the teenager still staring at the employment application.

''Is there a problem?'' Nick asked, steeling himself for the inevitable.

Robby cleared his throat. ''This says...um...under felony convictions...''

''That I spent the last fifteen months in the Pickaway Correctional Center.''

''You're an ex-con?'' Robby shifted in his molded plastic chair.

Nick nodded, not bothering to explain how he had voluntarily taken the rap for someone else, and in the process ruined his career and his reputation. He'd also apparently even ruined his job prospects at Farley's Fish Hut, one of the few places in town that had granted him a job interview since his release from prison a week ago.

''Cool,'' Robby exclaimed. ''I thought you looked kinda tough.''

A minimum-security prison was hardly Alcatraz, but Nick didn't have time to explain the subtle nuances of the penal system. ''Listen, Captain Robby,'' he said, checking his watch, ''I'm due to pick up my grandmother at the library in ten minutes....''

''No problem.'' Robby held out his hand. ''You start

training tomorrow at two o'clock. Welcome aboard, Mr. Chamberlin.''

Nick looked down at the flattened sheet of colorful cardboard in Robby's hand. ''What's this?''

''Your hat. All the crew wear one when they're on deck. It's required.''

Nick slowly reached for it. ''It doesn't look like a hat.''

Robby grinned. ''You have to put it together. It's shaped like a cod. That's our specialty. Oh, that reminds me, you'll need to memorize the menu list and our slogan. Oceans Of Fish, Fries, And Fun For Everyone.''

But Nick was still staring at the hat. So it had come to this. A thirty-three-year-old man with a college degree wearing a cod on his head and working his way up to the French fry machine. For five dollars and fifteen cents an hour.

Another Monday bites the dust.

THIS WAS Lucy Moore's lucky day.

She'd lost three pounds and found ninety-seven cents buried in her sofa. And she'd arrived at the Heritage Library employee parking lot just in time to save Gigi, Letitia Beaumont's pedigreed poodle, from a fate worse than death—the amorous attentions of a junkyard mutt cruising the nice side of town, where respectable dogs wore rhinestone collars and bows on their ears.

Not that Gigi couldn't use a little of the mutt's scrappy tenacity in her gene pool. So could her owner, the horrified and nearly hysterical chairwoman of the Heritage Library Foundation, Lucy thought as she gently shooed the mutt back toward his neighborhood—and hers. But she wisely kept that opinion to herself. Letitia expressed her eternal gratitude by promising to remember Lucy when the position of assistant senior librarian opened up.

Assistant senior librarian. It had a nice ring to it. Of course, not quite as nice as senior librarian, or even director of the Heritage Library. But not bad for a twenty-eight-year-old bookworm who grew up dirt-poor on the wrong side of Westview. And certainly better than her current position as staff librarian.

Lucy ran one hand over the smooth, green marble counter, warmed by the late-afternoon October sun slanting through the library windows. She couldn't wait to write to her brother Melvin and tell him all about it. Not that he would ever read it. He still returned all her letters unopened. Refused to take her phone calls. And generally irritated her with that masculine mix of bravado and martyrdom that always set her teeth on edge.

He'd been just as stubborn when they were growing up together. Of course, she'd been stubborn, too. She'd needed that mental toughness to survive the peer pressure on Bale Street. Avoiding the street gangs so she could earn a high-school diploma instead of a juvenile record. Spending all of her Saturday nights studying so she could win a full college scholarship to Ohio State University.

Through it all she'd always had her brother's support. Which was why she simply couldn't believe that now he expected her to sit back and do nothing while his life fell apart. He'd told her more than once to forget about him. To pretend she didn't even have a brother. To stay out of it, for her own good.

If she waited around for Melvin's consent, she'd never get anything accomplished. He simply worried too much. Recalled too many of her past mishaps. Like that annoying incident with the bleach. Pink underwear never hurt anybody. And weren't men of the nineties supposed to explore their feminine side?

It was time for Lucy to take matters into her own hands.

Maybe once she proved herself to him, he'd learn to loosen up a little. Melvin needed help. Her help. And she needed a street-smart sidekick to do the grunt work. Someone tough and tenacious. Dependable and desperate. Someone like the man Sadie Chamberlin boasted about every week at the library's Monday-afternoon meeting of the Merry Widows Book Club.

Now the only question was, how lucky could Lucy get?

"I can't wait to meet your grandson," she said to the silver-haired woman approaching the circulation desk. "I hope he's the right man for the job. I need someone who's not afraid to get his hands dirty. A man who's not afraid, period."

"He's perfect," Sadie Chamberlin replied, shifting the bulging library tote bag from one blue-veined hand to the other. "Very well-rounded."

"I can't pay much," Lucy warned for the third time that afternoon. "That's why every P.I. in Westview has turned me down."

Sadie smiled and reached over to pat Lucy's hand. "The money won't be a problem, dear. Nicky just finished doing a little work for the state, so he's in between jobs at the moment. I'm sure he'll be thrilled with anything you have to offer."

A little of Lucy's enthusiasm wavered. Nicky sounded almost too good to be true. She'd heard Sadie's glowing accounts of his youth, the summers spent in Westview, Ohio, with his adoring grandparents. Maybe Sadie saw him through rose-colored bifocals. Maybe Nicky Chamberlin was a no-account nerd. Just like Lester Bonn, the director of the Heritage Library. He snorted when he laughed, wore his pants a good two inches above the top of his shoes and whined about *everything*. A man—and she used that term loosely—only a mother could love. Or a doting grandmother.

"I want to see him before I make up my mind for sure," Lucy announced. "I always go by first impressions."

"Fine, dear. Now stand up straight. My grandson should be here any minute."

Lucy tucked a stray wisp of hair behind her ear. "Shouldn't we have some sort of signal."

"Signal?"

"A code word to let you know if I want to hire him. I mean, if he's not the right man for the job I wouldn't want to hurt his feelings." *Or make him cry.*

Sadie's faded blue eyes lit up. "A secret code! That's a wonderful idea. How about…'Mary, Mary, quite contrary, how does your garden grow?'"

Lucy wrinkled her nose. "That might be a little hard to work into the conversation. How about 'nice hat.'"

"Nicky doesn't wear a hat. Now his grandfather never went out of the house without one. Always a distinguished gentleman, my Nicholas. Did I tell you Nicky's named after him?"

Only about eight hundred times. Lucy smiled, warmed by Sadie's affection for her late husband. "You've mentioned it."

"Do you like spaghetti with meatballs?"

Lucy shrugged. "Once in a while. Why?"

"No, dear, I mean for our secret code."

Lucy nodded. "That's perfect. If I want him, I'll ask for your recipe for spaghetti with meatballs."

Sadie clucked her tongue. "No, that won't work. I never cook Italian."

"Well, we've got to come up with something—" Lucy said, before Sadie interrupted her with an excited whisper.

"Here he comes!"

Lucy looked toward the door and her mouth went dry. Nicky Chamberlin looked nothing like a nerd. No horn-rimmed glasses. No short, rail-thin body. No high-water pants. He looked big and bad, with short, jet-black hair slicked back, piercing gray eyes and a square, don't-mess-with-me jaw.

He looked like a man who could take apart a building brick by brick with his bare hands. And judging by the stubborn set of his chin, he'd do just that if he thought it was necessary.

A street-smart soldier for hire. Cheap.

Lucy told herself to remain calm as a bolt of excitement surged through her blood. She didn't want to act hastily. Or do anything impulsive. She needed to give this some serious thought. Weigh the pros and the cons. Check into his background, at the very least.

She took a deep breath, gazed directly into Nicky Chamberlin's gunmetal eyes and said, "Spaghetti with meatballs."

NICK DIDN'T THINK his Monday could possibly get any worse. Until a bee stung him on his way into the library. So now on top of a throbbing headache from his interview with Captain Robby, he had a throbbing pain in his right shoulder from the sting. And a wide-eyed librarian talking nonsense to him.

He turned to his grandmother, taking the heavy tote bag out of her grasp. "Ready to go?"

Sadie frowned up at him. "Nicky Chamberlin, I expect you to mind your manners and speak to Lucy."

"Who's Lucy?"

The librarian raised her hand.

He turned toward her, the embedded stinger in his shoulder grating against his shirt. Nick noticed her eyes first—

probably because they were big and round and staring openly at him—brown eyes flecked with gold and fringed with lush, dark lashes. He dropped his gaze from those eyes and found full, pink lips below a small, pert nose. Deliciously supple lips. Lips just made for kissing.

He mentally shook that image from his head, stunned to find himself fantasizing about Marian the Librarian. At least her hair looked the part, drawn back into an efficient knot at the nape of her neck. Except for those wisps of honey blond curls spilling over her smooth cheeks, teasing him with the promise of silky softness, tempting him to reach out and brush them off her face. Nick curled his hand into a fist to prevent him from doing just that.

He'd obviously been in prison too long.

"It's a pleasure to meet you, Mr. Chamberlin," she said at last, extending a slender hand for him to shake.

Nick reached out to grasp it, wincing as the stinger shifted painfully under his shirt at the movement. "Ow."

Lucy dropped his hand and frowned. "I'm sorry...I didn't mean to hurt you. My brother always believed a woman should be able to handle a firm handshake. I must have squeezed too hard." Her words sounded apologetic but her tone implied he was a wimp, and her big, brown eyes softened with disappointment.

Nick clenched his jaw, wondering why he cared about her opinion of him, especially when he'd stopped caring about anyone else's opinion a long time ago. Fifteen months to be exact. "No problem."

"What's the matter with you?" Sadie asked. "You look a little pale."

"Maybe he should lie down," Lucy suggested.

"It's nothing serious," he said. "It's just this damned—" he skittered a glance toward his grandmother

''—darned stinger in my shoulder. A bee got me on the way in.''

''You got stung?'' Sadie asked, her pale blue eyes clouding with concern. She looked at Lucy. ''Oh, dear. Now what?''

''Why don't I take him into the office and have a look at it?'' Lucy suggested.

Sadie smiled. ''That's a wonderful idea.''

''No,'' Nick insisted. ''I'll be fine.''

''Unless you're allergic,'' Lucy said. ''Then you could be dead in ten minutes. We've got a book called *How To Survive Venomous Bites and Stings.*'' She began pecking at the keys on the computer in front of her. ''I can see if it's on the shelf and look up the symptoms. We don't want to take any chances.''

''That's not necessary,'' he said.

''Now you look flushed,'' Sadie observed, laying her palm on his forehead. ''Maybe you should go rest for a while.''

''I think that's an excellent idea,'' Lucy exclaimed, and then turned toward the back office with a frantic wave.

''Look, this is ridiculous,'' Nick interjected as a short, balding man in a tweed jacket and bow tie joined Lucy behind the circulation desk.

''Is there a problem, Lucy?''

''As a matter of fact, Lester, there's a very serious problem.'' She pointed at Nick. ''This man just got stung by a bee and seems to be suffering some sort of reaction.''

''I never...'' Nick sputtered, but his grandmother placed a quieting hand on his shoulder, right on top of the stinger, turning his protest into a muted gasp of pain.

''You can see how much he's suffering,'' Lucy continued with a pitying glance at Nick. ''We can only hope he doesn't sue the city for damages.''

"A lawsuit?" Lester squeaked.

Nick rolled his eyes toward the tile ceiling and wondered if this Monday would ever end.

"Imagine the publicity, Lester," Lucy continued. "Vicious killer bees preventing entrance to the Heritage Library. Our patronage dwindles down to nothing. The staff protests the dangerous working conditions with a walkout. And the city council looks for a scapegoat."

"And I suppose everyone will assume this is my fault," Lester whined.

"Well, you are the library director," Lucy replied.

Lester nervously licked his thin lips. "What do you suggest we do?"

Lucy circled around to the front of the desk and hooked her arm through Nick's. "I'll take Mr. Chamberlin into the office so he can recover and rethink this pesky lawsuit idea of his. Can you handle the checkout line?" She motioned toward the long line of impatient patrons behind Nick and Sadie. "Mindy is still on break."

Lester nodded, his scanty mustache twitching nervously under his nose.

Sadie patted Nick's sore shoulder, and he had to steel himself to keep from flinching at the pain. "I'll just go visit with the members of my Merry Widows Book Club until you're through, dear," she said, nodding toward a small circle of white-haired women at a corner table. "Edith is telling her gall bladder story again, and I don't want to miss out on the good part."

Nick didn't say a word as Lucy led him into the cramped library office and closed the door behind them, flipping the lock. Then she pushed him gently down into a worn office chair, swiveling it away from the sight of Lester's half-eaten peanut butter and jelly sandwich lying on top of the desk. "Alone at last."

The hair on the back of Nick's neck prickled at her words. It had been a long time since he'd been alone with a woman, but he still recognized the subtle signs of physical attraction. The assessing glances. The flush of anticipation. The locked door. Then he reminded himself that this was a sweet, innocent librarian. And that he'd always had an overactive imagination.

She moved around to face him and he couldn't help but notice how well she filled out her caramel silk pantsuit. "Will you take your shirt off for me?"

Nick blinked at her. "What did you say?"

"Your shirt." She reached into the desk drawer, pulling out a pair of tweezers. "I'll remove that stinger for you."

Nick shook his head. "Forget it. I'm not going to sue."

"Oh, that," she said with a beguiling smile. "That was just a ploy to get you alone."

He swallowed. *Alone.* Had he been that obvious in his attraction to her? He took note of the way she was looking at him with that hopeful gleam in her brown eyes.

"Look, Marian..." he began.

"The name's Lucy. Lucy Moore. And don't be scared," she said, leaning over him as she briskly unbuttoned the front of his shirt. A stray wisp of her hair tickled his cheek. "It won't hurt too much."

His breath caught in his throat as her fingertips grazed against his bare chest. He stared up at her in disbelief as she peeled his shirt back over his shoulders.

"Now that I think about it," she mused, frowning down at him, "squeezing it might make it worse."

He shifted uncomfortably in the chair. "Squeezing *what?*"

"The stinger. I think you're supposed to scrape it off. Squeezing it injects more venom into the skin."

"Just get it out," he said, trying to ignore the fact that she'd just half undressed him.

She moved around to his back and tenderly traced one finger around the stinger. He closed his eyes at the bittersweet sensation.

"I'll have to use something else. Hold still."

He held still, every muscle relaxing under her touch.

"Ouch!" he suddenly yelped, inching away from her. "What was that?"

"My fingernail. I used it to scrape off the stinger. There," she said cheerfully, lightly patting his shoulder, "all better."

"It doesn't feel better," he grumbled as he heard her fumbling through the desk drawers.

"You really do have a low tolerance for pain, don't you? Now sit still, while I find some ointment to rub on it."

"Don't bother."

"It's no bother, and I promise it won't hurt." Her fingers gently smoothed a thick salve over his shoulder blade. "You might even like it."

His animosity faded. It wasn't her fault this was a Monday. Or that a bee had stung him. Or that he still couldn't figure out how to put together that stupid cod hat. She just wanted to help him. Besides, she was cute and quirky and harmless, if he overlooked how she'd scraped her fingernail across his back. And her touch did feel good as she slowly rubbed the ointment into his sore shoulder. Too good.

"Listen, Lucy, I need to go..."

"Your grandmother said I could have you."

"What?" He shot halfway out of the chair.

She pushed him back down. "Don't move. I still need to put on a bandage."

He unclenched his jaw as she briskly pressed a bandage across the sting. "I don't know what you and my grandmother have cooked up, but I'm just not interested.'' *Nice, Chamberlin, crush her poor little librarian's heart.*

Lucy walked around to the front of the chair, wiping her fingers with a tissue. ''But you haven't even heard my proposition yet.''

''I don't want to hear it.'' He leaned forward, his tone softening. ''It's nothing personal. I just don't have room for any complications in my life right now.''

''I'll pay you.''

Nick shook his head. She couldn't be that desperate. ''Sorry, I'm still not interested.''

She rolled her eyes. ''Your grandmother said you were stubborn, but this is ridiculous.''

''I'm not stubborn,'' he said. ''I'm a total stranger. You don't know anything about me.''

She tilted up her chin. ''Yes I do. Sadie's told me everything about you. I know your favorite color is blue. Your favorite meal is fried chicken with mashed potatoes and cream gravy and apple pie for dessert. And I know that you've got a scar on your left knee from a skateboard accident when you were eight years old.''

''Did you know I'm married?'' he lied, ready to put an end to her fantasies once and for all.

Lucy blinked. ''No...but that doesn't matter to me.''

''It might matter to my wife,'' he said indignantly.

She shrugged her slender shoulders, her brow furrowed. ''I don't see why it should. Unless your wife objects to us spending time together.''

''I think it's *how* we'll be spending that time together that she'll object to,'' he said, feeling more ridiculous by the moment for having this hypothetical argument. He didn't have a wife. Didn't want a wife. Not even as a figment of his imagination.

''This is pointless.'' Nick rolled his sore shoulder, trying to assuage the odd tingling sensation near the sting. "The bottom line is I can't give you what you want."

She frowned. "Why not?"

For a librarian, she was incredibly dense.

"Because I'm not attracted to you."

Something flickered in her brown eyes until she blinked it away. "Does that really make a difference?"

"To me it does." He knew she already suspected he was a wimp. Why not seal the impression? He clenched his jaw, forcing the words out. "I'm a...sensitive guy."

"I've noticed." She narrowed her brown eyes. "I realize it might get a little rough, but I really thought you could handle it."

He swallowed. "What kind of librarian are you?"

"A very desperate one at the moment."

"I've noticed." He plowed one hand through his short hair, almost wishing he was back in prison. Anywhere but with this luscious, love-starved librarian who wouldn't take no for an answer. "But don't you think it's just a little dangerous to ask perfect strangers to have sex with you?"

Her mouth fell open. And stayed open. Until Nick shifted uncomfortably in his chair and wondered if he might have possibly misunderstood her. Possibly made an asinine fool of himself. And just possibly turned this into the worst Monday on record.

"So let me get this straight," she said at last, her cheeks a rosy pink. "You think I want you to..." she moistened her lips with her tongue "to *pay* you to..."

Nick cleared his throat. Twice. "Isn't that what you meant?"

"No. Absolutely not. It never even crossed my mind." Her gaze fell to his bare chest and her blush deepened. "Will you *please* put your shirt back on?"

He pulled the shirt back over his shoulders, ignoring the

prickly sensation around the sting, while his fingers fumbled over each other in his haste to button it. "I'm sorry, I must have misunderstood...."

"Obviously," she said. Then a small smile tipped up her lips. "I suppose your wife would object to *that,* wouldn't she?"

Nick looked at her. "Well, actually...I'm not married."

Her smile faded. "You're not?"

He shook his head, his discomfort with the situation increasing at the same rate as the maddening itch on his shoulder. "I just wanted to make it clear that I'm not..."

"Interested," she finished for him. "I know. You've mentioned it at least five times now. I got the message loud and clear. You don't need to worry anymore, your virtue is safe with me."

"I—I don't want you to get the wrong impression," he stammered. "It's not that you're not appealing. I think you're absolutely gorgeous."

She narrowed her eyes in disbelief.

"All right, maybe not gorgeous. I mean...it's been a long time for me, so any woman looks pretty good...."

She raised one golden brow, daring him to bury himself even deeper.

Unfortunately, Nick could never refuse a dare. "You're very appealing for a librarian. I'm sure if the circumstances were different I might even be tempted myself...."

"Don't worry, Mr. Chamberlin," she assured him briskly. "The circumstances will *never* be different. I promise. Now can we get down to business?"

"Call me Nick," he said, absently rubbing his shoulder against the back of the chair. "And what business? Does my grandmother owe a small fortune in overdue fines?"

"No. This business is strictly personal." She held up

both hands. "And before you get the wrong idea again, let me explain. I want to hire you to help my brother."

"Do I have to wear a hat?"

"What?"

"Never mind. Sadie obviously told you I'm looking for work, but I've already found a job."

"Oh." Her face fell. "Then you really aren't interested?"

Maybe it was a sense of misplaced guilt for turning down what she'd never offered in the first place. Or the distracting itch in his shoulder. Or just a case of temporary insanity. Whatever the reason, he thought the least he could do was hear her proposition. "What kind of job is it?"

She hesitated, her teeth grazing her lower lip. "Well...I'd call it a research project, of sorts."

"Could you be more specific?"

She squared her shoulders and looked him straight in the eye. "My brother is in jail on arson charges. His trial starts in six weeks. Sadie told me you used to be some kind of crack investigator. I want you to help me find evidence that proves he didn't do it."

Nick opened his mouth and then closed it again. At last he said, "And just how am I supposed to do that?"

"By helping me find the person who did start that fire. And enough evidence to set Melvin free."

"Melvin. Melvin Moore," he said, rolling the name over his tongue. It sounded vaguely familiar.

"I'll pay you three hundred dollars a week," she added. "That pencils out to eighteen hundred dollars for six weeks' work. That's all I've got left in my savings account."

Three hundred dollars a week was considerably more than Farley's Fish Hut. Plus the fringe benefits: no hat and no Captain Robby breathing down his neck. He could do some respectable detective work instead of spending his days dishing up fish nuggets and tuna dogs. *Dogs.* Then it clicked.

"Your brother is *Mad Dog Moore?*"

She tipped up her chin. "His real name is Melvin."

"He torched the old Hanover Building downtown. Wasn't it some kind of historic landmark?"

"It still is," Lucy said. "Most of the damage was due to smoke and water. That building can still be restored. Melvin knew it needed work when he bought it eight months ago. He planned to turn the ground floor into a sports bar and renovate the upper floors into apartment units. So why would he burn it down?"

"For the insurance money," Nick replied, remembering the articles he'd read in the newspaper. One of the few pleasures of prison life. "He took out a hefty policy on that old building only a few weeks before the fire. It's a simple open-and-shut case."

Lucy tipped up her chin. "Somebody obviously framed him."

"Is this the same man who drove his motorcycle into traffic court and asked the judge if he'd like to go for a spin?"

"That was a long time ago. He's changed."

"And didn't I read that he hot-wired the mayor's car as part of a gang initiation?"

"He was only fifteen at the time," Lucy explained. "Besides, everybody makes mistakes."

Nick knew that only too well.

She folded her arms across her chest. "If you don't want to take the job, I'll find someone who will."

"Maybe you should do that. Just how much did my grandmother tell you about me?"

Her expression softened. "A lot. She's very proud of you."

"Did she tell you where I've been for the last fifteen months?"

"She said you had a job with the state."

He shook his head. Leave it to Gram to make his prison stay sound like a career opportunity. "I suppose you could say that. I was at the Pickaway Correctional Center."

"Oh, were you a guard?"

"Actually I worked in the laundry."

"But I thought prisoners usually worked in the laundry."

"That's right."

It took a moment for his words to sink in. "You mean you're an ex-convict?"

He nodded, waiting for the usual reaction. It would be interesting to see how she wiggled her way out of her job offer now.

"But that's wonderful! You'll be perfect."

He blinked. "I will?"

"Of course. Whoever framed Melvin isn't going to surrender easily. It could get rough out there. I need someone tough and cagey on my side. Someone who thinks like a criminal."

"Don't you even want to know my crime?"

She shook her head. "It doesn't matter. If you were only there for fifteen months, it couldn't be that bad, right? Besides, we need to concentrate on Melvin. That is, if you'll take the job."

He sighed. "You really think he's innocent?"

"No," she replied. "I *know* he's innocent. Despite all his brushes with the law, Melvin has never lied to me. My brother swears he didn't start that fire. And now I intend to prove it, with or without you."

Nick closed his eyes. He admired her loyalty, but the

word of a miscreant like Mad Dog Moore didn't hold much weight with him. Which left him with two choices. He could take this woman's money when he *knew* her brother was guilty. Or he could let someone else take her money, while he mopped the deck at Farley's Fish Hut. With a paper cod on his head.

He reached back to scratch the persistent itch on his shoulder blade. Maybe he should just take the job and prove to her that nobody but Mad Dog could be guilty. Prove it to her before she spent every cent she had on a worthless cause. Or before she let some greedy, incompetent private eye bleed her dry.

"All right, I'll do it," he said, trying to ignore that guilty twinge in the pit of his stomach. Knowing he'd never take the case if Farley's Fish Hut weren't his only other alternative. "But I can't make you any promises."

"I don't need any promises," she said cheerfully. "Just results."

"Speaking of results, I don't think this stuff is working." The ferocious itch spread in an ever-widening circle around the sting. "Just what kind of ointment did you put on my shoulder?"

Her brown eyes widened with concern. "Why? Isn't it any better?"

"No. And the itching is making me crazy." He rubbed the back of his shoulder against the cracked vinyl padding on the chair.

She sighed. "That's too bad. I thought it might work."

"You thought what might work?"

"The peanut butter. It was all I could find." She smiled innocently at him. "You know that old saying Put Butter On A Burn. I thought maybe peanut butter might work for a sting."

Nick closed his eyes and took two deep breaths. "You put peanut butter on my shoulder?"

"From Lester's sandwich. I rubbed it in really well."

He didn't know whether to laugh or rip his shirt off and beg her to rake her fingernails across his back again. "I'm not allergic to bee stings, Lucy," he said with a preternatural calmness. Even now he could feel the huge, itchy, red welts rise up over his back and shoulder. "But I am allergic to peanuts."

"Oh, Nick, I'm so sorry. I shouldn't have experimented on you." Lucy nibbled her lower lip. "I hope this won't make you change your mind about working for me."

"It's not your fault," he said with a sigh of resignation. "It's a Monday."

Despite his discomfort and his lingering doubts, he'd given his word. He couldn't walk away now. Or run, as some small part of his brain was urging him to do at the moment. Warning him that Lucy Moore just might be the most dangerous woman he'd ever met.

He shoved that ludicrous thought back where it belonged, into his overactive imagination. Marian the Librarian didn't have a dangerous bone in her delectable body. Her most risky escapades probably involved eating raw cookie dough and not rewinding rented videotapes before she returned them.

He didn't have anything to worry about. *She was a librarian, after all.*

How dangerous could she get?

2

"THIS IS ILLEGAL. I can't believe I'm letting you talk me into this," Nick muttered as his gaze quickly scanned up and down the darkened street.

"We're not *technically* breaking in," Lucy said, wishing he'd stop worrying so much and just jimmy the lock already. Or let her do it. Her fingers itched to give it a try. For the first time in her life, she'd be participating in an adventure instead of just reading about it. "I really do have a key to this place somewhere. I just can't seem to find it."

She peered over his shoulder, watching him wiggle the nail file she'd given him into the keyhole. "I'm guessing you didn't serve time for breaking and entering. Why is this taking so long?"

"Because I'm giving myself a manicure!"

"You don't have to yell at me."

"I am not yelling at you," he said, slowly enunciating each word. "I'm all yelled out from your slamming that car door on my foot."

"I already told you that was an accident. And for somebody who said he didn't want to attract any attention, you certainly made enough noise."

Lucy heard him swear softly under his breath, but she wasn't sure if the oath was directed at her or at the stubborn lock. That antihistamine he'd taken earlier was obviously making him cranky.

"I never should have agreed to come here tonight," he

muttered, more to himself than to her. "We should have waited until tomorrow to search this place. On a nice, safe Tuesday."

"I have to work tomorrow," she said. "Besides, somebody might see us roaming around in here during the day." Somebody who might not like her snooping around the Hanover Building again. Maybe the same person who kept making crank phone calls to her apartment in the middle of the night and leaving footprints in the flower bed outside her bay window.

She watched Nick's back muscles shift under his chambray shirt as he picked the lock. She felt safer now, with him by her side. And more than a little guilty for not telling him about the possible danger. But she didn't know for certain if the phone calls and the footprints and the eerie sensation of someone watching her were connected to the fire and Melvin. And he hardly seemed like a man who would trust a woman's intuition. Especially hers.

"So what if somebody does see us?" he asked, twisting the file in the lock. "Your brother still owns this place, right?"

Lucy considered the question. "Well, actually..."

But a sharp, metallic click interrupted her. Nick turned to her and smiled. "We're in."

She followed him into the building, inhaling the faint, residual odor of acrid smoke in the cool, musty interior. Old places like this had always held a fascination for her. Full of untold stories of the people who had come and gone. She loved to imagine the events played out here over the last hundred years.

She sighed inwardly, thinking of Melvin's unfinished story. Hopefully she and Nick could steer it in the right direction. Because Lucy always hoped for happy endings.

"Stay here," Nick ordered. "I'll check out the upper floors."

He left her side before she could tell him she had no intention of becoming a bystander in this investigation, although she admired his take-charge attitude, his professional demeanor. And she really liked his smile, realizing it was the first time she'd seen it today. She especially liked that tiny cleft in his chin that made him seem almost friendly.

Unfortunately, his command hadn't sounded very friendly. It had sounded brusque. Impatient. And downright bossy. It reminded her of similar commands she'd reluctantly obeyed as a girl. Melvin's commands, delivered in an equally aggravating manner. *You stay put, Lucy. And stay out of trouble.* He hadn't trusted her to evade the bad crowd that was always so easy to find on Bale Street.

He'd never let his baby sister tag along with him and his rough-and-tumble gang of misfits, either. Boys like Snake and Buzz and Weasel. Melvin didn't want her tangled up in his wild adventures.

Her brother had always worried about her. When she was six, she'd developed severe asthma, and suffered from chronic bouts for several years. Her wheezing terrified him. Especially since he was responsible for her while their mother worked double shifts at the potato chip factory. Their father spent most of his time at the corner tavern, in between visits to his parole officer.

Melvin and Lucy had soon learned to depend on each other. She'd help him with his homework, while he'd administered her medication and kept her supplied with library books. She spent most of her childhood curled up with a book, keeping company with a fascinating array of fictional characters.

Even in high school, she preferred the heroes in her

books to the aimless boys hanging out on the street corner. Too many of her friends had gotten sidetracked by a handsome face. Bale Street was filled with women who had loved the wrong man. They'd traded their dreams for broken marriages and dead-end jobs and children to support.

But not Lucy. She'd woven her own fantasies, inspired by the feisty, indomitable characters that filled the pages of her books. She knew that a better life than Bale Street was possible for herself and her family. A life of respectability and opportunity and promise. So she played by all the rules.

After her parents died in a car crash when she was twenty, Lucy only had Melvin left. And her dreams. It was a long, hard climb, but she was almost there. Only it wouldn't mean anything without her brother.

It just wasn't fair.

He'd made a break from his troubled past, but now faced twenty years in the state penitentiary for a crime he didn't commit. She was determined to face any obstacle, take any risk to set him free. Especially since she'd always wanted to do more than read about daring escapades and spine-tingling adventures.

Lucy wasn't going to play by the rules anymore.

She walked toward the south end of the Hanover Building, to the makeshift apartment Melvin had lived in during the renovations. Stopping in front of the door, she was surprised to find it slightly ajar. The fire hadn't come close to this part of the building and the last time she'd been here, shortly after his arrest, this door had been locked.

She pushed it open, assuming the police had come back at some point for more so-called evidence. And done a very sloppy job of it, she observed, as she moved into the middle of the disarray Melvin used to call his living room. The love seat and both armchairs lay overturned on the scuffed linoleum floor, foam stuffing spilling out of the jagged tears in the fabric. Glossy posters hung haphazardly on the wall, and dry cereal was piled in sugary pyramids on the kitchen counter next to the empty boxes.

All courtesy of the Westview police, who obviously didn't bother to clean up after themselves. No doubt they assumed a former resident of Bale Street wouldn't notice the difference.

Lucy tried to swallow the lump in her throat, but it wouldn't budge. As she turned into the tiny, utility kitchen for a glass of water, she heard footsteps outside the apartment door.

"Nick?" she called out, hearing something scrape against the closed door and then more footsteps.

"Nick?" Lucy called again, only louder this time.

No answer. No sound at all now outside that door. Lucy's breath caught in her throat as she heard the distinct shuffle of feet overhead. Nick checking out the upper floor. Which meant…

Which meant somebody else was down here with her. Somebody who didn't want her to know it.

Lucy plastered her back against the wall next to the door and frantically dug through the purse slung over her shoulder for some kind of weapon. She found a barrette, a pack of gum, a bookmark and an old throat lozenge. But nothing really useful like a gun or a baseball bat. Unfortunately, Nick still had her nail file.

She heard a low grunt on the other side of the wall and then more footsteps. Her fingers suddenly curled around another object inside her purse. It might not stop whoever was out there, but it could possibly slow him down long enough for her to escape.

She took a deep, shaky breath as more sounds emerged from beyond the door. She had two choices. Stay trapped in here while the intruder planned his next move, or confront him, using the element of surprise.

I can do this…I can do this…I can do this. Lucy pulled the impromptu weapon out of her purse and took a step toward the door. Then two. Then three.

The sounds had stopped again, but the hair prickling on her arms told her someone was still out there. She pulled the door open, wincing at the creak of the hinges, and peered out into the murky expanse. The silence seemed ominous now, the shadows malevolent, the air really dusty.

She sneezed—twice. Her gut twisted and her heart slammed against her ribs as she moved quickly away from the door, edging along the hallway wall. Even through her fear she sensed a frisson of excitement zipping through her body. The realization that her first adventure was just about to begin.

She could only hope it wouldn't be her last.

She froze as the soft patter of footsteps echoed just around the corner. They were steady now; determined. Her arms trembled slightly as she held them out straight in front of her, her weapon at the ready. She resisted the urge to turn and bolt, to flee instead of fight, and then a strange detachment settled over her. When the intruder suddenly rounded the corner, bearing down on her, she didn't scream or throw up or faint like she'd always imagined she might when confronted with danger. She just screwed her eyes tightly shut and squeezed the nozzle under her fingertip.

A yelp of pain ripped through the silence, followed by a thud. Lucy cracked open one eye to see the intruder hunched down on his knees, his face bent to the floor.

"Gotcha!" she exclaimed, ready to strike again if he so much as moved one of those bulging muscles. She tightened her hold on the travel-size can of hair spray and aimed the nozzle toward his dark head.

The man took a deep, shuddering breath. "Are you some kind of deranged lunatic?"

She opened both eyes and stared down at him in horror. "Nick?"

"Of course, it's me," he roared. "Who were you expecting...Jack the Ripper? I think you've blinded me. What is that stuff? Pepper spray?"

"No, it's hair spray. Super Hold. Unscented. I'm pretty sure it's nontoxic."

He slowly straightened up, then reached for his shirt pocket. He fumbled inside it for a moment before pulling out a handkerchief. "*Pretty sure.* Well, that's a big relief."

He wiped the sticky hair spray out of his eyes. Then he swabbed at his wet forehead, the dark strands of his hair stiff and glistening in the slivers of moonlight streaming through the grimy windows. "Don't you think you've already done enough damage to me for one day?"

"You don't understand. I heard footsteps." She dropped her voice down to barely a whisper. "Someone's in here with us."

"Yeah, well, if it's the hair police, I'm safe."

"Just listen," she implored.

He cocked his head to the side and listened for all of two seconds.

"I still don't hear anything."

"That's because you're yelling at me again. You've probably scared him off by now."

He stuffed the handkerchief back into his shirt pocket. "See how much easier that is than assaulting people with hair care products."

Lucy resisted the childish urge to stamp her foot on the floor. *Why wouldn't he take her seriously?* "But it might be the arsonist, returning to the scene of the crime."

He shook his head. "You've been reading too many

mystery novels. That hardly ever happens. If you did hear something, it was probably just a mouse."

Then the distinct sound of loose bricks cascading to the floor echoed from one dark corner of the building.

"Loud mouse," she said dryly. "Do you want me to check it out?"

He got slowly to his feet. "No, you and your hair spray have done enough harm for one night. I'll handle it. You stay here."

Stay here. Again. Lucy pressed her lips together. Hadn't she just shown him that she could take care of herself?

But Nick didn't stick around long enough to see if she obeyed his order. He turned and moved silently along the wall that led to the far corner.

Adrenaline still pumped through her veins and her can of hair spray still had at least one or two good shots left in it. Nick needed backup and she needed to redeem herself for spraying the wrong guy. And prove to him that she could hold her own in this investigation.

So she crept after him, unable now to even see his silhouette in the deepening shadows, but priding herself that her footsteps were just as soundless as his. Only one day in the cloak-and-dagger business and she'd already disabled a man who outweighed her by at least sixty pounds and was now tracking down a bad guy as if she'd been doing it for years. Lucy Moore—master spy.

Her fantasy came to an abrupt—and bruising—halt when she bumped up against something big and hard and immovable. Something that made her heart leap to her throat. Something that grabbed her tight and wouldn't let go.

Nick.

"Sorry," she gasped as he whipped her around so fast, her head snapped against the wall. He pressed her back hard against it, the full length of his powerful body pinning her in one easy motion. Her breath caught in her throat at the sheer strength of him. The painful grip of his hands on her shoulders loosened, but he didn't let go. She wriggled against him, her hands trapped against his hard chest.

"Don't move," he whispered, his lips brushing against her ear.

"Did you see something?"

He nodded, listening intently, his hands still grasping her shoulders and his rough cheek grazing her soft one. He stood there for several long, silent minutes. Then he lifted his head just far enough to look into her eyes, his mouth just a hairbreadth from her own. His heart beat a rapid tattoo beneath her fingertips as his steely gaze flicked to her mouth.

Lucy swallowed, mesmerized by the expression on his face. He leaned toward her, the motion so slight she couldn't even be certain he'd moved at all. Then he pulled his head back abruptly and his flinty gray eyes narrowed. "What are you trying to do to me?"

"I'm not doing anything to you," she whispered. "I'm just trying to help."

A muscle flickered in his jaw. "Lady, I don't need your kind of help." Then he pulled away from her, robbing her of the warmth of his body and any wild notions she might have entertained about Nick treating her like an equal partner in this investigation.

"Maybe you don't," she whispered, trying not to sound disappointed. "But Melvin does. Do you think I'm going to just stand around, just *stay put,* when I could help find the proof we need to set him free?"

He closed his eyes. "Lucy...we're not going to find any..."

A strangled cry echoed through the building as a wiry figure shot up from the corner and barreled through a pile of cardboard boxes as though pursued by demons. Nick spun around, one long arm extended to clothesline the man around the waist as he sped by, knocking the air out of him. The intruder went down like a rock, his eyes wide open and panicked as he gasped for air.

Nick towered over him, one foot pressed against the side of his neck, almost daring him to move.

"We caught him!" Lucy exclaimed.

The man on the floor swallowed convulsively, his prominent Adam's apple bobbing in his throat, then pointed one shaky finger in the direction of the corner. "R-r-rat," he breathed. "A big one."

Lucy squinted down at him. "Weasel?"

Nick looked at her. "He said *rat.*" Then a hopeful gleam lit his eyes. "Lucy, if you're afraid of rats, why don't you wait for me in the car? I can handle this."

"I'm not afraid of rats," she informed him evenly. "I'm not afraid of Weasel, either." She smiled down at him. "Hey, Weasel, how's it going?"

"Hey...Lucy," Weasel said, his panicked expression fading as he blinked up at her. His admiring gaze traveled slowly up the length her body. "Wow, you look great. Really hot."

"Thanks," she replied, a blush warming her cheeks as she self-consciously smoothed down her blue mohair sweater.

Nick shifted his weight, until Weasel's eyes bulged out and odd gurgling noises bubbled out of his throat.

Lucy frowned up at him. "You're choking him. Get your foot off his neck and let him get up."

Nick eased off the pressure. "First, he answers a few of my questions." He glared down at him, looking as if he'd rather squash him than interrogate him. "How do you know Lucy?"

Weasel took a deep, unhampered breath and then his mouth twisted into a smirk. ‘‘She’s my woman.’’

BY THE TIME Nick abandoned the temptation to grind his heel down Weasel’s windpipe, Lucy had the guy up off the floor and resting comfortably in one of the wounded armchairs in Mad Dog’s apartment.

Nick watched while she crooned over him, dabbing at the microscopic scrape on his forehead and reassuring him that the rat wouldn’t make any sudden appearances. And if it did, she vowed to annihilate it with her hair spray.

Lucy the Terminator. Or in this case, *Exterminator*.

Nick rubbed one hand over the thick stubble on his jaw and wondered how he’d let his life get so out of control. He thought he could handle starting over. Playing it safe while he rebuilt his life. Structuring some sort of future, however bleak.

He thought he could handle Lucy.

Until those brief, tantalizing moments he’d had her backed against the wall. Her body soft and curvy in all the right places. Her silky hair smelling like vanilla. Her full, pink lips slightly parted and so tempting that his body tightened at the memory.

Then he shook the image from his head. At least she didn’t seem to notice his short departure from reality. Probably because she couldn’t keep her eyes or her hands off that…Weasel. Nick’s gaze narrowed as he studied the man sprawled in the chair. He wore a black mesh muscle shirt and faded blue jeans with a trendy rip in each knee. His brown hair was neatly pulled back into a short ponytail. A colorful tattoo adorned each brawny arm.

He certainly hoped the guy wasn’t serious about that ‘‘She’s my woman’’ crack. Not that Nick wanted any claim to Lucy himself. His life was screwed up enough without involving himself with a kooky librarian—or any woman, for that matter. He didn't want that kind of responsibility, that kind of distraction. Not until he resolved his own problems, his own disappointments.

But Lucy could certainly do better than this lowlife.

"That feels so good," the lowlife said, his head lolling against the back of the chair. His eyelids fluttered shut as Lucy massaged his temples. "You've got magic fingers, Luce."

Nick stalked over to them. "It's time for Lucy and her magic fingers to take a rest. You've got some explaining to do."

Weasel cracked one eye open. "Are you still here?"

Nick leaned down, his voice low and menacing. "Here and in your face until you tell me what I want to know."

Lucy scowled at him. "Nick, have a little compassion. Weasel hit his head on the floor when you tackled him. He's got an awful headache now, possibly a concussion, as well as a nasty cut on his forehead."

"Maybe you should rub some peanut butter on it."

She tipped up her chin. "Maybe *you* should apologize."

She couldn't be serious. "Me? Apologize? I'm the good guy, remember?" He pointed to Weasel. "He's the bad guy."

Weasel held both hands up in front of him in mock surrender. "Hey, I'm innocent until proven guilty. I know that much."

Nick snorted. "I'll just bet you do. So let's lay out the incriminating evidence we've got against you so far." He counted off the offenses with a flick of his fingers. "Number one—breaking and entering into private property. Number two—stalking. Number three—"

"That's not fair," Lucy interjected, laying one hand on

Weasel's burly shoulder. "Give him a chance to explain. And quit treating him like a common criminal."

Nick shrugged. "Hey, if the handcuffs fit…"

"It's all right, Luce," Weasel said, patting her hand. "I'm used to it." Then he arched his neck to look up at her. "But does Mad Dog know you're hanging around with a cop? I visited him at the jailhouse yesterday and he didn't say a word about it."

"Nick's not a cop," she assured him. "He's my private investigator."

Weasel turned to scowl at him. "He *smells* like a cop."

"You're way off base," Lucy said with a smile. "Tell him, Nick."

"I'm a cop," Nick replied, thoroughly enjoying the brief flare of panic in Weasel's eyes. Then he saw the puzzled look on Lucy's face. "All right, I'm not a cop," he admitted. "Not anymore."

"What's that supposed to mean?" she asked. "I thought you were an ex-con."

"I am."

"But that doesn't make any sense…."

Nick's jaw clenched. "Do we have to talk about this right now?"

Weasel clasped his hands behind his head. "No time like the present. So tell us, how did you land the big house? I'm guessing you're a dirty cop who got caught. Am I right? Was it a little money under the table? Some racketeering?"

"Actually, I killed a guy for asking too many dumb questions."

Lucy's brown eyes widened with apprehension. "You… killed a guy?"

"No," Nick replied, wishing he'd kept his mouth shut. Now she'd want to know all about him. He resisted the ridiculous urge to confide in her. To make her understand what he didn't fully understand himself. To assuage his sense of loss and betrayal. But this wasn't the time and certainly not the place. Besides, it would be a totally selfish act, and stupid. He couldn't tell her, or anyone. No matter what she thought of him now.

"I got released from duty for an ethics violation and served fifteen months in prison for possession of stolen property," Nick snapped. "Can we get on with the investigation now?"

Weasel shook his head. "The only thing worse than a cop is a *dirty* cop. Get rid of him, Luce. You don't need his kind of help."

"Yes I do," she said firmly. "This means he can think like a criminal *and* like a cop. He's just the man for me."

Her words thawed some frozen place deep in his soul, warming him from the inside out. Where others saw failure and disgrace, Lucy saw possibilities. She believed in him despite his past, believed he could prove her brother innocent.

Too bad he'd have to let her down. Because despite Lucy's optimism, Mad Dog was still the most obvious suspect. The *only* suspect. And the sooner she accepted that fact, the better.

Which was why he didn't tell her about the matchbook. The dirty, dilapidated, charcoal-smudged matchbook he'd found stuck under the floorboard after she'd nailed him with the hair spray. It had once been white, etched with now barely legible gold lettering. The police must have missed it while sorting through all the debris. And Nick was almost certain any prints they'd find on it would belong to Mad Dog Moore.

So he kept it hidden away in his shirt pocket. The last thing he wanted to do was get her hopes up. She was already the most dangerously optimistic person he'd ever met.

"Look, we've wasted enough time here already," Nick said gruffly. His gaze fixed on Weasel. "Ready to tell us your story?"

Weasel smirked up at him. "Once upon a time..."

"Weasel, please," Lucy murmured, gently squeezing his shoulder.

"All right," he said reluctantly. He looked up at Nick, his gaze serious now, but still belligerent. "What do you want to know?"

He wanted to know everything. Why Weasel chose tonight to break into the Hanover Building. What he was looking for. Why Lucy obviously liked him so much. Why it bothered Nick that she did.

"What's your connection to Lucy?" he asked, his curiosity getting the better of him.

"We go way back."

Nick propped one foot on a corner of the chair, his forearm resting on his knee. "Care to elaborate?"

Weasel leaned back in the chair. "I already told you, she's my woman."

"In your dreams, pal," Nick said, certain she wouldn't associate with a two-bit hood like Weasel. Nick had seen enough of his kind during his years on the force. Crass. Disrespectful. Lazy. He probably knew Lucy from the library. Sometimes bums hang out there.

"Hey, she wanted to marry me, *pal,*" Weasel retorted. "But I'm a confirmed bachelor, so I had to turn her down."

Lucy planted her hands on her hips. "You might want to mention that I was only ten years old at the time."

Weasel feigned disappointment. "You mean the offer isn't good anymore?"

She smiled. "You're a confirmed bachelor, remember?"

Then she turned to Nick. "Actually, Weasel and I do go way back. We both grew up in the same neighborhood, on Bale Street. He lived two doors down and used to hang out with Melvin."

Bale Street? Somehow he couldn't imagine Lucy living in that decrepit, lawless part of town, although Weasel would fit right in.

"So what are you doing here now?" Nick asked him, casting a purposeful glance toward the scorched north wall. "Reliving the good old days? A little looting? Some breaking and entering?"

"*I've* got a key," Weasel said with a sneer. "How about you, Officer? Trying to impress the lady with some breaking and entering of your own?"

"It was my idea," Lucy interjected. "I couldn't find my key, but my nail file worked just as well."

Weasel shook his head. "Your key wouldn't have worked at all, Luce. All the locks have been changed."

"Who changed them?" Nick asked, looking from Weasel to Lucy and back again. A faint, reminiscent gnawing in the pit of his stomach told him he didn't want to hear the answer. The same gnawing he used to get on the police force when something unexpected, and really bad, was just about to happen. And the guilty look on Lucy's face didn't make him feel any better.

"It must have been Vanessa," she mused.

He was almost certain he didn't want to know, but the cop in him made him ask the question. "Who's Vanessa?"

"Vanessa Beaumont," Weasel supplied. "She's Mad Dog's woman. Or at least she used to be until he became eligible for twenty years in the state pen. Princess Vanessa likes the bad boys, but only if they're available."

"So who gave her permission to change the locks? Mad Dog?"

Weasel looked at Lucy. "You didn't tell him?"

Nick closed his eyes as his stomach clenched and twisted. After a Monday like this, he'd probably get an ulcer. And he'd name it Lucy. "Tell me what?"

She cleared her throat. "I must've forgotten to mention it in all the excitement." The wail of police sirens nearby almost drowned out her next words. But not quite. "Neither Melvin nor I actually own this building."

"YOU HAVE THE RIGHT to remain silent," the police officer droned. The harsh red glare of the flashing lights illuminated the stark, implacable expression on Nick's face. "Any statement you make can be used against you in a court of law. You have the right to consult with an attorney...."

Lucy couldn't let another minute go by without at least trying to rectify this mess. *Her* mess. If only he'd given her a chance to explain! But Nick had simply stared at her when she'd admitted the truth. Shocked into silence, he'd allowed Weasel to slink away and the police to arrive, ignoring her suggestion that they make a run for it, as well. By the time the officer assessed the situation and easily apprehended Nick and Lucy, the shock on his granite face had faded to grim resignation.

"This is all a big misunderstanding," she interjected, cutting off the uniformed officer's recitation of the Miranda warnings.

"Shut up, Lucy," Nick said evenly.

The officer, a young man with a boyish face dusted with freckles, scowled at Nick before swinging his gaze to her. "Would you like to make a statement, ma'am?"

"Yes I would," she replied.

"No she wouldn't," Nick countered.

She stifled a sigh of exasperation. Didn't he realize that

they could end up spending the night in jail over a simple misunderstanding? That might not bother him, but she still had a reputation to maintain.

"Yes, I'd like to make a statement, Officer," she insisted. "Several, in fact."

A pale blue sedan pulled up behind the police cruiser. The driver cut the lights and then lumbered out of the car.

"What have we got, Madison?" the new arrival asked, hitching up the baggy slacks of his wrinkled brown suit. His craggy face and thinning gray hair marked him in his late fifties. His world-weary attitude and the shoulder holster Lucy glimpsed beneath his jacket marked him as a plainclothes police officer.

Officer Madison nervously flipped through the notepad in his hands. "Looks like we interrupted a burglary in progress, Lieutenant," He held up Lucy's nail file. "They picked the lock with this."

She reached for it. "That's mine. I'd like it back, please." She knew they probably needed it as evidence, but it was one of a kind and had a lot of sentimental value. The fingernail file had belonged to her grandmother, also named Lucy, and had the letter *L* artfully etched in the genuine mother-of-pearl handle.

"All in good time," the man said, slipping her nail file back into the evidence bag. Then his gaze slid to Nick, and he stiffened with recognition. "Been a long time, Chamberlin."

"Lieutenant Delaney," Nick acknowledged with a slight nod of his head. "You're working late tonight."

"I'm pulling a double shift. We're a little shorthanded down at the station. How long have you been—" Lieutenant Delaney cleared his throat "—back in town?"

"About a week."

The lieutenant eyed the Hanover Building. "You're keeping busy, I see."

Lucy took a step forward. "It's not what it looks like, Lieutenant. Nick didn't want to break into the building, but I forced him."

"Lucy..." Nick's voice sounded low and dangerous, but she ignored it, as well as the incredulous expression on Officer Madison's freckled face.

"He thought I owned this building. I told him I had a key." She caught her lower lip between her teeth. "Well, actually, I do have a key. It just doesn't fit the lock anymore." She could feel Nick's piercing glare fixed on her. "Did I mention that I want to file a complaint against the Westview police department?"

There was a pregnant silence.

Then Lieutenant Delaney looked at Nick. "Is she for real?"

"Unfortunately for me, yes."

Lucy bristled at the exchange. "Yes, Lieutenant, I'm for real. So is my brother, the man your police department wants to send to prison for a crime he didn't commit. And then—" she pointed toward the building "—you add insult to injury by destroying his apartment. Melvin's personal belongings are my responsibility now. And I intend to see that..."

"Melvin?" Lieutenant Delaney interjected, his bushy gray brows furrowed with confusion.

"Mad Dog Moore," Nick supplied. "Meet his sister, Lucy."

The lieutenant's wrinkled forehead cleared, and to Lucy's astonishment—and chagrin—the man looked like he was trying to hide a smile.

"I think I'm beginning to understand the situation." He turned to Officer Madison. "I can handle it from here,

Johnny. You go back to the beat. Oh, by the way—'' he hitched up a thumb ''—good job.''

He waited until the police cruiser edged away from the curb and into the deserted street before turning back to Nick and Lucy.

''He's a good kid, but fresh from the academy. I try to keep an eye out for him.'' He looked at Nick and his face sobered. ''Like your grandfather did for me. I...uh...never got a chance to offer you my condolences. Nicholas Chamberlin was a great cop. I'll never forget everything he did for me.''

''Thanks,'' Nick said stiffly.

''That's why I'm gonna let you two off the hook,'' Lieutenant Delaney said, handing Lucy the bag containing her nail file, ''this time. The building's secure and no harm's done. So stay out of trouble from now on, and don't make me sorry I cut you a break.''

Lucy's knees went weak with relief. A night in jail might be a whole new adventure but it certainly wouldn't look good on her résumé, or help her secure the promotion she wanted so badly. ''Thank you, Lieutenant. You won't be sorry. I'm still new at this, but I'm a fast learner. And I can almost guarantee you that we won't break any more laws during our investigation.''

Nick groaned, covering his eyes with one hand.

''Good luck to you, Chamberlin,'' Lieutenant Delaney said, clapping Nick on the shoulder. ''Looks like you're gonna need it.''

3

HE'D TELL HER TONIGHT.

Nick tugged at one end of the black bow tie around his neck, unfurling the crooked knot for another attempt at tying it on straight. He never should have accepted Lucy's invitation for dinner. But she'd been so apologetic about the incident with the police and so determined to make it up to him. In the end, she'd simply worn him down. To the point that he'd agreed to wear a tuxedo, because she wanted to take him somewhere special.

Nick evened out the ends of the tie, then carefully began to knot it. He doubted this monkey suit would soften the blow when he told Lucy that he couldn't pursue the case because there simply was no case. He'd spent the last three days researching the Hanover Building fire and Mad Dog Moore and the insurance angle. He still needed to talk to his friend and former partner, Cole Rafferty, who had led the fire investigation, about any possible leads, new or old. But that was just a formality. Cole had obviously come to the same conclusion. Mad Dog Moore set that fire and now he had to face the consequences.

At the moment, those consequences almost seemed preferable to facing Lucy when he told her to accept her brother's guilt and get on with her own life. Maybe he'd take away all her cutlery beforehand, just to be on the safe side.

With an impatient yank, Nick loosened the mangled bow

tie once more, leaning closer to the small mirror in the attic bedroom. He'd used this room on visits to his grandparents' house ever since he was eight years old. His own parents, busy with careers and active in state politics, had shipped him off to Ohio every summer. As he grew older, it seemed only natural that Nick would follow in the footsteps of the grandfather he loved and admired so much. He attended the police academy in Cleveland, then joined the Westview force, a rookie the same year his grandfather was promoted to police chief.

It all seemed like a lifetime ago. His parents still lived in Oregon, exchanging cards with him at Christmas and birthdays. But they'd never invited him back home since his conviction.

Nick sighed. He knew he couldn't stay with Gram forever. This visit had already extended beyond his original intentions. Maybe he needed to take his own advice and get on with his life. Look for an apartment. Another job. A remote control with a mute button.

Because if he had to listen to one more song from *Oklahoma,* Gram's favorite musical, he was going to take his Glock 9 mm out of retirement and shoot the television set. She watched the videotape at least three times a day and listened to the soundtrack CD in between.

Not that living with Gram didn't have its advantages. He loved her cooking and her company. Enjoyed running errands for her and tinkering with her car. But when he caught himself humming ''Surrey with the Fringe on Top,'' he knew it was time to start looking for a place of his own. A very *cheap* place.

He had to admit he'd miss his grandmother. Even if she did periodically drive him crazy. Because she also loved him unconditionally. She had been too torn apart by her husband's death a year and a half ago to even comprehend the events surrounding Nick's arrest and conviction. She'd always just accepted his vague explanation of making a few mistakes.

She'd never criticized or censored him, just offered her unending support and a promise that she'd be waiting for him when he got out. She'd also sent two dozen home-baked cookies every week, making him the most popular guy in his cell block.

Her unquestioning acceptance of his confession of the crime sometimes made him wonder if she suspected the real truth, but didn't want to face it. Prison had given him ample time to go over the event that changed his life forever. To wonder what would possess his grandfather, a highly respected former chief of police, to steal that marijuana from the evidence room at the police station. He'd come up with dozens of scenarios, but none of them made sense. And now, almost two years later, he still had more questions than answers.

Finally satisfied with the bow tie, he stared at his reflection in the mirror. The tux still fit after all this time, the black lapels neatly pressed and in stark contrast to the crisp, white, pleated dress shirt. He looked like the maître d' at Château Pierre. Maybe that's where Lucy planned to take him for dinner. Maybe they'd have a job opening.

The last time he'd dined at the Château Pierre had been two years ago at his grandfather's retirement party. The Westview Police Department had spared no expense to celebrate the exemplary thirty-five-year career of Police Chief Nicholas Chamberlin. He died a short four months later with his reputation and his secrets still intact.

Nick intended to keep it that way.

"Don't you look handsome," Sadie exclaimed as he descended the staircase that led into the living room. "And wait until you see Lucy." His grandmother swept one arm toward the stone fireplace, where Lucy stood studying the framed photographs on the mantel.

"Isn't she a dream, Nicky?"

More like his worst nightmare. Then she turned and smiled at him, and his heart stopped beating for one paralyzing moment.

What happened to his librarian?

Her honey blond hair swept down in gentle waves around her shoulders, framing her face and deceptively innocent smile. A shimmering ice blue cocktail dress clung to her slender figure, revealing surprisingly seductive curves in all the right places, curves that caught and held his attention longer than good manners or political correctness allowed. But Nick couldn't help himself. She looked delicious and wanton and more dangerous than she ever had before.

"Isn't she, Nicky?" Sadie asked.

He swallowed. "Isn't she…what?"

"A dream," Sadie insisted.

He nodded. A dream. He was dreaming. That had to be it. Or delusional. That hair spray she gassed him with probably wasn't hair spray at all, but some toxic, slow-acting nerve gas. He closed his eyes. Remember the hair spray, he told himself. The peanut butter. The other disasters Lucy Moore could lead him to with just one crook of her little finger.

He opened his eyes and breathed again. After tonight, he'd never see her again. After he told her about the overwhelming amount of evidence confirming Mad Dog's guilt, she'd never *want* to see him again.

"Hold still, dear," Sadie said, reaching up to straighten his tie. "There. Perfect. Now go stand next to Lucy. I've got to have a picture of the two of you."

"This isn't the prom, Gram," he protested. "And I'm sure Lucy made reservations. We don't want to be late."

"Don't worry," Lucy said. "We have plenty of time."

"Lucy, scoot over closer to Nicky," Sadie ordered, pulling the camera out of the case. "Nicky, relax. You look like you're facing a firing squad. Lucy, hook your arm through his. That's right. Now stand a little closer together. Closer..." Sadie held the viewfinder up to her eye. "All right everybody, smile! Say...spaghetti with meatballs."

"Take off the lens cap first," Nick advised.

She removed the lens cap and then frowned down at the 35 mm camera in her hands. "It seems like I'm forgetting something else."

"Film?" Lucy guessed.

"Batteries?" Nick asked.

Sadie snapped her fingers. "Oh, I remember now. Goodness, how could we forget? Nicky, go into the kitchen and get Lucy's corsage."

"Corsage?" he echoed.

"Yes, dear," Sadie said with a sly wink in his direction. "The corsage you ordered from the florist this afternoon. It arrived while you were dressing and I put it in the refrigerator for safekeeping."

"A corsage!" Lucy clasped her hands together. "Oh, Nick, you shouldn't have."

She was right. He shouldn't have. In fact, he hadn't. But he couldn't very well admit that now. Not with Lucy looking at him like that, flushed with pleasure. His grandmother, however, would have some explaining to do when he got home tonight.

But first he needed to figure out how to pin the delicate champagne rose corsage on Lucy's dress without actually touching her. He stood close to her, his head bent as he tried to pin on the flower, resisting the urge to look down her dress. Her silky hair brushed against his cheek and his fingers kept grazing the soft, warm skin beneath her collarbone as he fumbled with the pin, jabbing himself three times.

"Got it," he said at last, stepping away from her so fast, he tripped over the andiron next to the fireplace.

"Smile," Sadie chimed, snapping the picture just as he fell at Lucy's feet.

And it wasn't even a Monday.

LUCY'S GRIP TIGHTENED on the steering wheel as she drove through downtown Westview and fumed silently.

Three days. Three whole days without a word from him about the investigation. Nick sat in the passenger seat beside her, quiet, aloof. Already she could read him as well as any book. He was shutting her out of the case. Making her *stay put* while he continued to search for clues without her.

The aromatic scent of the corsage weakened her outrage. It almost made her feel guilty about pretending to take him out for dinner. How did he know champagne roses were her favorite? She'd never expected it, especially from Nick. He didn't seem like the romantic type.

He did, however, seem like the irritating type. The strong, silent, let-me-handle-everything type. The type who didn't bother to tell her he used to be a cop. *A dirty cop.* She still couldn't believe it. He seemed so noble. So forthright. So annoyingly honest.

Nick might not be a cop anymore, but he acted like a cop, thought like a cop. And if he thought he could exclude her from this investigation, then she was more determined than ever to prove him wrong.

"We're here," she announced, pulling into the crowded parking lot and cutting the engine.

Nick peered through the windshield at Westview's new civic auditorium, a gleaming brick-and-steel structure bathed in the numerous spotlights scattered over the manicured grounds. "I see that. The only question is why? I thought you were taking me out for dinner."

"Just stay close behind me and follow my lead," she said, hopping out of the car before he could question her further.

"Lucy!"

But she just kept walking, hearing Nick's muttered curses and hurried footsteps echoing behind her. Her heart raced in her chest as she approached the front entrance. She'd never done anything like this before in her life. It was calculated. Conniving. Simply wonderful.

She took a deep, calming breath and assessed the situation. A grim Jeeves at twelve o'clock, checking the invitations of the guests as they filed through the door. Security guard at two o'clock. He was well armed, but pudgy, and had to be at least sixty years old. Lucy was almost certain she and Nick could outrun him if it became necessary.

She ascended the first two steps, ready to put her plan into action, when Nick grasped her by the elbow.

"Do you mind telling me what's going on?"

Lucy shook her head. "Not now. They'll get suspicious. Just play along." She wiggled out of his grasp and moved up to the top step.

"Your invitation, madam?" the doorman requested, holding out one white-gloved hand.

"Of course," Lucy said, reaching into her beaded purse. She pulled out a card of ivory parchment and handed it to the doorman. Her pulses pounded as he looked at it.

"Mr. and Mrs. Reginald Van Whipple," he read aloud, then began checking his invitation list.

"That's right. And what is your name?"

"Alfred, ma'am," he murmured, his gray brow furrowed as his gaze moved up and down the list.

"Alfred." Lucy turned to Nick with a bright, phony smile. "Remember that name, Reggie. We'll want to tell Letitia how fortunate she is to have such a competent man on staff." She leaned forward, resting her hand on Alfred's forearm. "Reggie and I just flew in from Palm Springs. It was an exhausting trip, but we just couldn't let Letitia down. And it *is* all for charity."

"Yes, of course..." Alfred muttered. "I'm sorry, Mrs. Van Whipple, but I can't seem to find your name on Mrs. Beaumont's list."

"Oh, dear, we simply *must* be there. We're always invited to all the best parties. Dear Letitia and I go way back. Did she ever tell you the story of how we first met eleven years ago? It was March third, a rainy Friday..." she began, eliciting impatient groans from the gathering crowd behind them.

"Perhaps the omission was just an oversight," Alfred said. "After all, you do have an invitation."

"Indeed, we do," Lucy said, her knees weak with relief. "Reginald, tip this darling man."

Nick looked at her. "What?"

"A tip, darling." Would it kill him to help her out a little here? "Just a little something to show Alfred our appreciation."

Nick reached for his wallet. "Anything for you, my darling Cruella. But all I've got is a twenty."

"Very good, sir," the doorman said, neatly plucking the bill out of Nick's hand. "Please enjoy your evening."

Lucy sailed into the ballroom foyer. She pulled a stem from a large vase of white carnations while she waited for Nick, snapping off the blossom with her fingernail.

"That was quite a performance, Mrs. Van Whipple," Nick said, joining her. "What do you do for an encore?"

She stuck the carnation in the buttonhole on his lapel. "I dance," she replied, pulling him onto the ballroom floor before he could protest.

"So who are the Van Whipples?" he asked as he circled his arm around her waist, clasping her hand in his.

Lucy smiled up at him. "We are, for tonight anyway. Mr. and Mrs. Van Whipple are the lead characters in one of my favorite mystery novels, *High Society Sleuths.*" Then she scowled. "And her name is Penelope, not Cruella."

"My mistake." He skillfully maneuvered them around an elderly couple performing an impromptu tango.

"So how exactly did Reginald and Penelope get an invitation to this shindig?"

"We're crashing. The Beaumonts do a lot of charity work, and tonight they're hosting a fund-raiser for the Friends of Westview Association. Letitia Beaumont also heads the Heritage Library Foundation. She often uses the library staff for personal business, so I wasn't surprised when she asked me to address the invitations."

"Enter the Van Whipples."

"Only because I couldn't afford the one-thousand-per-plate donation needed to finagle an invitation."

He whistled low. "A thousand dollars per plate? Must be some great food." Then he looked at her. "Don't you feel the least bit guilty, Mrs. Van Whipple, for enjoying a dinner you don't intend to pay for?"

"Don't worry," she told him, nestling her head against his sturdy shoulder as they swayed to the slow, languorous music. "I intend to contribute something."

She closed her eyes, aware of the pressure of his broad hand on the small of her back. *No harm in enjoying a brief respite from their mission while waiting for phase two to begin,* she thought to herself as they floated across the dance floor. No harm in pretending to enjoy Nick's arms around her, either. Or the bulge of muscles beneath her fingertips. Reminding her of his strength. His power. His endurance.

"Ouch," he exclaimed as she missed a step, grinding the spiked heel of her shoe into his foot.

"Oops, sorry," Lucy apologized, embarrassed at her lack of coordination. Reginald Van Whipple never complained about a little discomfort. Even when his wife accidentally shot him in the leg, mistaking him for the villain. "Are you all right?"

"I'm fine," he replied. "Just promise me that Reginald doesn't suffer some horrible, torturous death before the story ends."

"Of course not. You worry too much," Lucy murmured next to his ear. "Relax. Trust me."

"Said the spider to the fly."

She didn't understand his cynicism. They'd made it through the door. Now they could enjoy the party until it was time to put her plan into action. "Maybe I just want to show you a good time. Maybe I thought you could make some connections here that might benefit the case."

"Listen, Lucy. We need to talk about the case."

"I agree," she said. "You've been shutting me out of the investigation, Nick. I'm intelligent, resourceful. All I want is a little respect."

"I do respect you," he said softly against her ear. "As a librarian. You are not, however, Penelope Van Whipple, high society sleuth. And you don't seem to realize that all these silly games of yours could lead to serious trouble."

"I know this isn't a game," she replied. "My brother's future is at stake. I may be all that stands between his freedom and twenty years in the state pen."

"So do you mind telling me how crashing this party to sip champagne and dance the night away accomplishes that?"

"Not at all," she said. "My instincts tell me Vanessa knows something about the fire. But we need to get close to her to find out."

"Vanessa Beaumont? The current owner?"

Lucy nodded. "She financed Melvin's purchase and renovation of the building. According to the contract, if he missed more than two payments, an option clause allowed the ownership to revert to her."

"So while Mad Dog sits in jail awaiting his trial, Vanessa exercised the option clause," Nick deduced. "Not a very understanding girlfriend, is she?"

"Ex-girlfriend," Lucy clarified. "She broke up with him after his arrest. Vanessa isn't exactly the loyal type."

"How did they ever get together in the first place?"

She sighed. "They met at a literacy reception at the Heritage Library. Letitia brought Vanessa and I invited Melvin. Unfortunately, he's attracted to thin, gorgeous and shallow."

"And Vanessa's here tonight?" he asked, looking eagerly around the room. A little too eagerly in Lucy's opinion.

"Yes."

"So why not just give Vanessa a call and ask to talk about the case?"

"I tried that already."

"And?"

"And she said no. We're not exactly in the same social circle."

"So you're hoping that rubbing sequined elbows together tonight might convince her to open up?"

"Of course not. I'm hoping my donation will convince her."

Nick raised a brow. "I was under the impression you don't have much money."

"I don't. But I'm not donating money."

"What then?"

She grabbed his hand, pulling him off the dance floor. He still didn't seem ready to join in the spirit of the occasion. Maybe he was hungry. "Shall we go help ourselves to the appetizers?"

"Not until you finish answering my questions."

"They have shrimp cocktail. And I think I saw some buffalo wings."

"Lucy..."

"Or a vegetable tray if you're trying to stay in shape. Did I mention how nice you look in your tux?"

"Thank you. Did I mention how good you are at evasion?"

She smiled. "Thank you."

He shook his head. "I didn't mean it as a compliment."

She looked wistfully over at the crowded buffet table. "Why don't we finish this discussion after we eat?"

The squeal of a microphone forestalled his reply as a portly gentleman in a white tie and tails stepped onto the raised platform in the center of the room.

Just in time.

Nick moved a step closer to her, his tone softening. "Why are you afraid to tell me about your donation, Lucy? Is it...I mean, there's nothing...illegal about it, is there?"

She blinked up at him in surprise. "Of course not. Whatever gave you that idea?"

"Maybe because you're acting so guilty about it."

The man on stage tapped the microphone several times. "Testing one, two, three..."

"That's silly. I don't feel the least bit guilty."

"So then tell me," he insisted.

"Tell you what?"

A muscle flickered in his jaw. "What you're donating to lure Vanessa into discussing the case."

"You."

He gaped at her. "What?"

Lucy reached up to straighten the white carnation on his lapel. "Didn't you understand my answer?"

"Didn't you understand my question?"

"Ladies and gentlemen, may I have your attention..."

"You're my donation, Nick. Now I don't have a lot of time to explain, so just go with the flow. I already signed you up. You can't back out now."

He frowned at her. "Signed me up? For what?"

"...it's now time for that exciting event you've all been waiting for...."

She gave his hand an encouraging squeeze. "Don't look so apprehensive. It's painless, I promise you."

"I don't like the sound of this," he announced. "What exactly did you get me into?"

"...if the usherettes will please escort all the gentlemen wearing white carnations to center stage."

Lucy smiled up at him. "The bachelor auction."

A perky usherette hauled Nick off before he could say another word—which was fortunate for Lucy, judging by the look on his face. That wait-until-I-get-my-hands-on-you look. And she knew without a doubt that the only place his hands wanted to be were wrapped around her neck.

His look only confirmed her earlier decision not to tell him about the bachelor auction in advance. Sadie had warned her that Nick didn't like to call attention to himself. Tended to be touchy about public exhibitions. Hated surprises.

But Sadie hadn't said anything about an aversion to charitable donations. As Lucy watched him reluctantly ascend the stage, she knew she'd made the right decision. He probably just avoided events like this out of a sense of self-preservation.

Because what woman wouldn't want a man like him?

Not her, she told herself firmly. She needed to concentrate on the investigation, not her love life. Besides, he was an ex-con, which made him definitely off-limits. She hadn't clawed her way up from Bale Street to a respectable life and career to throw it all away for a pretty face.

She wanted to fall in love—someday. With a man who met all her requirements. He needed a good career, a steady income, a spotless background. No Bale Street bums for her. Unfortunately, Nick didn't fit into any of her required categories. He was unemployed, broke and had a criminal record as well as a reputation as a dirty cop. She'd seen enough women on Bale Street dragged down by the men in their lives.

Not that she ever had to worry about choosing between him and her dreams of success. Nick had made it crystal clear in the library office last Monday that she couldn't interest him if she danced buck naked on top of his bed. Those weren't his exact words, but she didn't need to be hit over the head with a book of rejection lines to get the hint.

However, from a perfectly objective viewpoint, she couldn't help but notice how easily he surpassed the other bachelors gathered on the stage. He wasn't movie-star handsome. His nose crooked just a little in the middle, as if a break never quite healed properly. That, combined with the small scar on his square chin and his flinty gray eyes, gave him a subtle edge of roughness that appealed rather than frightened.

His impressive height made him stand literally head and broad shoulders above the rest. She swallowed, remembering the sight of those bare, brawny shoulders, and that wide expanse of hairy chest that gradually narrowed to a lean waist and taut, rippling stomach. The feel of those hard muscles flexing beneath her fingertips...

Lucy swallowed again, her throat uncomfortably parched. Then she glanced over to the other side of the stage, hoping she wasn't the only woman to notice how easily Nick Chamberlin stood out in this crowd of pampered blue bloods.

She wasn't disappointed.

Vanessa Beaumont sat at a cordoned table adjacent to the stage, sharing a shrimp cocktail with her adoring father while her eyes feasted on Nick.

She'd taken the bait.

Lucy let out her pent-up breath, relieved that her assessment of Melvin's old girlfriend had proven right on target. Vanessa had grown up rich and pampered, cutting her capped teeth on premed preppies and boys from Snob Hill. Now she preferred men with more raw edges. Tough and gritty, with a hint of danger about them. Men like Nick.

She experienced a momentary twinge of uneasiness watching Vanessa drool into her napkin. Nick certainly wouldn't be duped by Vanessa's blatant sexuality and millions of dollars in the bank. He had more sense and integrity than that.

Didn't he?

"Good evening," the emcee bellowed into the microphone. "I'm Ralph Rooney, president of the Friends of Westview Association, and I'll be your emcee. Welcome to our third annual fund-raiser and bachelor auction."

The crowd erupted into applause.

"I'd like to thank Harold and Letitia Beaumont for hosting the event this year. According to the association's police liaison, Lieutenant Ed Delaney, last year's donation has made it possible for the police department to continue the Protégé Project. This is a project that gives at-risk juveniles and inner-city residents temporary employment. It provides them with a paycheck, plenty of job experience and networking opportunities for those individuals with the drive and the gumption to succeed."

Ralph waited for the applause to fade before he continued. "We have several participants in the Protégé Project working here tonight. They're employed as valets, coat-check clerks and bartenders. So tonight you can actually see your donations at work."

Lucy politely applauded with the rest of the crowd until she saw Letitia Beaumont squinting in her direction. She surreptitiously moved behind a potted palm.

"Now the moment you've all been waiting for," Ralph announced. "Ladies, have we got a fine selection of bachelors here for you to choose from this evening."

Piercing wolf whistles and shouts from the female audience members filled the air.

"Over here, big boy!"

"Pump it up, fellas!"

"Let's see some skin!"

The Friends of Westview Annual Fund-Raiser and Bachelor Auction generated a lot of money and drew women from all over the state, most of them successful, aggressive career women who weren't afraid to go after what they wanted—or whom.

Several of the bachelors on stage grew fidgety. Some pranced and preened to the appreciative cheers of the crowd of ravenous women. Nick just stood there and glared at Lucy.

She tugged up the corners of her mouth with her fingers, motioning for him to smile.

"The rules are simple," Ralph continued. "The highest bidder gets her man for a date on the town. For simplicity and convenience, the bachelors will be notified of the arrangements through the Friends of Westview office secretary."

A muted drum roll sounded from the orchestra pit. "So without further ado," Ralph bellowed, "it's time for our bachelor auction. And to kick off tonight's affair we've received a special request from the audience—" he winked in Vanessa's direction "—to begin with this bachelor right here." Ralph clapped his hand on Nick's shoulder.

The cheers and applause grew even more raucous.

Ralph conferred for a moment with Lucy's reluctant donation and then checked the information card she'd sent in yesterday. "We've got a fine specimen here, ladies. Mr. Nick Chamberlin. A real man's man. Nick enjoys moonlit walks, candlelight dinners and cuddling."

Nick visibly cringed.

"Do I hear a bid of two hundred dollars?"

Several women screamed their bid at once. So many of them wanted Nick, it was hard for Lucy to keep track as the bidding quickly escalated.

"Five hundred!"

"Seven fifty!"

"One thousand dollars!"

Lucy couldn't even see Vanessa anymore as a throng of potential buyers, young and old, milled around the edge of the stage. She rose on her tiptoes, scanning the crowd through the palm fronds as the emcee whetted their appetites even more.

"Turn around, Nick, and let the ladies see the whole package," Ralph Rooney insisted.

A soprano chorus of appreciative oohs and aahs mingled with wolf whistles from the crowd of women.

The emcee egged them on. "Any woman who wins a date with this bachelor will certainly have her hands full. Take a good look, ladies, before you pass up this hunk of USDA prime beefcake."

"Fifteen hundred dollars," screeched a frantic matron next to Lucy.

"Fifteen seventy-five," a hoarse debutante called out.

Lucy stumbled over the potted plant and almost got trampled in the process.

"Sixteen fifty."

"Seventeen hundred."

Gradually the frenzied pace of the bidding slowed until only a few, determined voices remained in the fray.

"Going once," the emcee called at last.

Lucy caught her breath and held it.

"Going twice."

Nick mouthed a few words at her from the stage that at first she interpreted as "I'm going to kill you." But he couldn't be *that* upset about an innocent bachelor auction. He probably meant he was going to *bill* her. And, of course, she intended to pay him for a good night's work.

"Sold! For two thousand dollars," Ralph Rooney announced, "to Miss Vanessa Beaumont."

"THE MONEY GOES to a good cause," Lucy stated, driving through the lighted streets of Westview. She wondered how much longer Nick could last without saying a word.

Maybe he was a little bit upset after all.

"It's not like I sold you into bondage. It's only one date."

Nick shifted in the passenger seat, piercing her with his merciless gaze.

"Look on the bright side. Most men would give a year's salary to go out with Vanessa," she continued. "Although personally, I don't see the attraction. In my opinion, she's a total flake. I can't figure out what guys find so appealing about her. I mean, unless you're into big breasts, long legs and flawless skin, what is there to like? She's shallow, greedy and possessive."

He just kept staring at her.

"Don't you think this silent treatment is just a bit childish?" she exclaimed, unnerved by his unblinking perusal. "If you're upset about what happened tonight, just say so."

"I'm upset about what happened tonight."

Lucy smiled. "That's better. It's not healthy to keep your feelings all bottled up inside, Nick. Now that we've got that out into the open, we can concentrate on our next step. I think we need to expand our list of suspects. Vanessa is my choice as pyromaniac of the year, but I overheard talk tonight that Ralph Rooney made an offer to buy the Hanover Building. Maybe we should keep an eye on him, too."

He met her suggestion with more tight-lipped silence. His attitude bewildered her. Tonight had been a major success. Vanessa had fallen right into their trap. But Nick certainly didn't act very happy about it. Maybe he resented Lucy springing the bachelor auction on him without warning. Or maybe he simply didn't like taking orders from a librarian. As a former police detective, he was probably used to running the show.

She looked over at him, anxious to make amends with her new partner. "So, Nick, do you have any ideas?"

He drew himself up in the seat, one hand gripping the dashboard so tightly, his knuckles turned white. "Just one." The softly spoken words belied the menace in his tone. "I'm resigning from this job. Effective immediately."

Her mouth dropped open. "You can't do that."

He settled back against the seat. "Just watch me."

She turned off the street into a restaurant parking lot, certain he couldn't be serious. Quitting meant giving up, and Lucy simply didn't believe in giving up. Giving up meant spending your life on Bale Street. Giving up meant watching your brother serve twenty years in state prison. Giving up meant forfeiting your dreams. It simply wasn't an option.

She cruised up the drive to the fast-food menu box. "You're not thinking clearly. Where could you find a job more exciting than this one?" she asked as she rolled down her window. "You're probably just hungry. You'll feel better after we eat."

"Ahoy, mate!" crackled a voice from the speaker. "What's your pleasure?"

Lucy leaned her head out the window. "I'll have an order of fish nuggets, large fries and a Farley's Hurricane shake. Chocolate."

"Would you like candy sprinkles or minimarshmallows with that Hurricane, ma'am?"

"Sprinkles." She turned to Nick. "What do you want?"

He stared disconsolately at the bright neon Farley's Fish Hut menu box, topped by a large, plastic cod. "I just want to wake up from this nightmare."

"Don't you want something to eat?" she asked, feeling a twinge of guilt. "I promised you supper tonight and you haven't eaten a thing. They've got great fish nuggets here. Or you might want to try the cod fingers. Cod's their specialty."

Nick paled. "So I've heard. Thanks anyway, but I think I'll pass."

Lucy pulled up to the drive-thru window and gave her money to a pimply-faced teenager with a cod hat on his head.

''Hey, Nick,'' the teenager called, leaning down to peer through the driver's side window. ''Good to see ya, buddy.''

Lucy turned to her stony companion. ''Do you know him?''

''That's...Captain Robby,'' he replied, acknowledging the teenager with a short nod.

Lucy took the bulging, greasy sack Captain Robby handed her and then rolled up the window. The aroma of fish and fries filled the car. Maybe the food would work its magic on Nick. There was nothing like a sack full of salty, saturated fats to bring her out of a bad mood.

''Mmm,'' she breathed. ''Doesn't it smell heavenly? Are you sure you're not hungry?'' She held up a fried fish nugget. ''I'm willing to share.''

He turned his gaze away from her food and stared out the window. ''No, thanks. I've lost my appetite.''

''That's too bad,'' she said, munching on a French fry. ''So where did you meet Captain Robby?''

''Listen, Lucy,'' he began, raking a hand through his hair. ''About my resignation... I might have been a little hasty.''

She looked up from her Farley's Hurricane shake. ''Really?''

He hesitated a moment, his gaze fixed on the colorful dancing cod decorating the take-out sack, then he nodded. ''Really. I'm not quite ready to resign yet.''

''I knew you'd see it my way,'' she said, cheerfully munching on a crispy fish nugget. ''And you'll see the wisdom of this date with Vanessa, too. You just need a little time to adjust to the idea.''

''Time,'' he echoed, leaning back against the headrest as he closed his eyes. ''Yeah, that's what I need...a little time.''

THIRTY MINUTES LATER, Lucy was humming under her breath as she unlocked the door to her apartment, proud of her part in tonight's success. *Mission accomplished.* With a well-paired investigative team like her and Nick, the real arsonist didn't stand a chance.

"I'm home," she called out, closing the door behind her and hanging her purse on the coat tree.

A plaintive meow sounded from under the sofa.

Lucy bent down to coax the black cat out of its hiding place. "Hello, Sherlock. Sorry I took so long, but I brought you a treat."

She pulled a lukewarm fish nugget out of the crumpled take-out bag, peeling the crispy layer off the top. Then she crumbled the flaky white meat into a small plastic bowl. "From Farley's Fish Hut. Your favorite."

The cat just looked up at her and meowed again.

"What's the matter, Sherlock?" Lucy asked, scooping him up into her arms. "Did we get another one of those phone calls?"

She looked over at the answering machine and saw it blinking at her.

Not again.

With a sigh of resignation, she punched the message retrieval button. The first call sounded uncomfortably familiar: a man breathing heavily while he called her name in an eerie singsong voice. Like Tiny Tim with a head cold. Creepy, but probably harmless.

It was the second call that made her heart jump into her throat.

"Hey, Luce. It's me, Melvin. We've got trouble."

4

Melvin "Mad Dog" Moore sat in the visitors' room of the county lockup the next morning and glared at his sister. Usually his baleful expression and brawny build sent both men and women scurrying across the street to avoid crossing his path. But Lucy just smiled at him, knowing full well his bark was worse than his bite.

"You look wonderful," she said, sitting across a wide wooden table from him, a twelve-inch-thick pane of Plexiglas between them. She took in his wavy blond hair, dark brown eyes and smooth-shaven cheeks. "I'm glad you got rid of the beard. I've always loved that dimple on your chin."

"It's not a dimple," Melvin growled. "It's a scar. I got it in a fight at Harrigan's Bar."

"Who was your opponent? A plastic surgeon?"

His hard mouth tipped up in a smile. "All right. So I can't keep any secrets from my baby sister. Just don't let that dimple story get spread around. Remember, I know the truth behind those rolled-up socks you used to wear. And I don't mean on your feet."

"I was a sophomore in high school and underdeveloped for my age." Lucy crossed her arms in mock outrage. "I can't believe you'd resort to blackmailing your own sister."

"Prison has been a bad influence on me."

Her smile faded. "What's wrong, Melvin? You said there was trouble."

"My lawyer quit yesterday." He sighed. "Looks like you spent all that money on him for nothing."

She sat up straighter on the hard wooden chair. "He can't just quit! Your trial is in less than a month. I'll sue him. I'll report him to the state bar association. I'll picket in front of his office until he agrees to represent you again."

Melvin shook his head. "Hey, if he's not on my side, then I don't want him. The last thing I need is for my own *lawyer* to believe I'm guilty."

"Is that what he said?" she asked, knowing that her brother valued loyalty above all else. So did she. When you grew up on Bale Street, rife with crime and double-dealing, trust and loyalty were priceless commodities.

He shrugged. "Close enough."

She hit the scratched tabletop with her fist. "This is so unfair! You are not guilty. And I intend to prove it to that slimy lawyer and everybody else in this town."

He folded his beefy arms across his chest. "That's the other thing I wanted to talk to you about."

The hairs on Lucy's neck prickled at his tone. It wasn't that she was afraid, just a natural reaction to twenty-eight years of being bossed around by a big brother. A six-foot-three, two-hundred-and-twenty-pound big brother.

"Well, we both know you're innocent," she began.

"And?" he prompted.

"And I won't rest until I prove it. I'll find another lawyer...delay the trial...hire a psychic. I know we can find the evidence to clear you."

He arched a thick, blond brow. "We?"

She swallowed. "I've hired someone to help me with the investigation."

"A man?"

"Nobody you know," she said quickly. Melvin had never quite accepted that she was old enough to date. "He's retired from the police department and lives with his grandmother. He's perfectly harmless."

Melvin snorted. "Weasel's already told me all about this *harmless* friend of yours. Nick Chamberlin. Thirty-three-years old. Ex-con. Sex maniac."

Her mouth dropped open. "He's no sex maniac. I can guarantee you that."

"And what's that supposed to mean?"

"Well, he got stung by a bee," she began.

"Sounds painful, but hardly a permanent disability. Are you telling me this bee sting has affected his love life?"

"Not exactly."

"Then what, exactly?"

She decided to skip the rest of the story. "It means Nick Chamberlin isn't interested in my body. Only a paycheck. My relationship with him is strictly business."

"Not according to Weasel. He told me the guy practically drools every time he looks at you. Weasel's worried about you, Luce, and so am I. Especially since I can't keep an eye on you from in here."

"I can take care of myself," she said softly.

He rolled his eyes. "Right. As long as you've got your nose buried in a book. But this isn't fiction, Lucy, it's real life. You don't know what, or who, you're up against."

"Nick is on our side. He's one of the good guys."

"I have a feeling *good old Nick* is on the side that can pad his bank account. He's after your money," he said, his face darkening, "and anything else he can get. Forget him, Lucy. Forget me. You've got your own life to live. You don't need me to drag it down."

"You're my brother," she whispered, her throat tight. "The only family I've got left. And I'm not about to let you spend the next twenty years in prison for a crime you didn't commit."

"You don't need to worry about that. I've got a plan."

She didn't like the sound of that. "A plan?"

He nodded. "If it all works out, I won't need another lawyer."

"So are you going to fill me in?"

"No way. The only reason I contacted you at all is so you don't send any more money to that lousy lawyer. The less you know, the better."

She rolled her eyes. If he was going to start that nonsense again, she'd never get anything accomplished. So she resorted to a tactic that had worked on him since she was eight years old. "Actually, I already know all about it. Weasel told me."

Melvin scowled at her.

"You do not."

"Do, too."

"Do not."

"Do, too."

"Do not!"

She shrugged, feigning unconcern. "Fine. You don't have to admit it. But I'm really hurt that you would try to keep something like this from me." She sniffed for good effect. "I'm your sister. At least Weasel understands that I have a right to know."

"Man, he did tell you!" He shook his head in disbelief. "How could Weasel let you get mixed up in something like this? I never should have told him my plan to bust out of here."

She blinked. "You're *what?*"

Melvin narrowed his eyes. "So you really didn't know," he accused. "Damn! I hate it when you do that to me, Lucy."

She leaned closer to him. "Melvin, are you crazy?"

"Yeah. Crazy to stick around this place for so long. To

even think I stood a chance of an acquittal. You don't know what it's like in here, Luce. My cellmate, José, talks to his invisible friend. The bedsheets are giving me a rash. And I've named the spiders living in my toothbrush holder Harvey and Doris.'' He raked his fingers through his hair. ''I'm cracking up, Luce. I've got to get out of here.''

She wanted him out of there, too, but planning a jailbreak definitely wasn't the answer. It was all so unfair. He'd been ready to make something of his life. Instead of leaving the old neighborhood, he had a plan to make it better. Provide jobs for a decent wage and better housing for reasonable rent. And just like Lucy, he wasn't a quitter.

Lucy couldn't let him give up now.

''Melvin,'' she whispered, ''if you try to escape, they'll lock you up and throw away the key.''

''They'll have to catch me first.''

''But you shouldn't have to run away. You haven't done anything wrong.''

He leaned forward and said softly, ''I know you believe life should be fair, Lucy. Maybe it's that way in books, but I realized a long time ago that sometimes we have to make our own happily-ever-after.''

''Just wait a little while before you do anything rash. I know Nick and I can find the real arsonist.''

''The only thing Nick Chamberlin is going to find is trouble if he lays one finger on my little sister. I know his type. At the moment, I'm surrounded by them. He's not going to solve this case. He's just going to clean out your bank account.''

''You've got it all wrong,'' she said, her mind racing for a way to convince him to delay his escape attempt.

''I'm right about this, Lucy,'' he countered. ''I want you to dump this guy.''

''All right.''

He blinked. ‘‘What did you say?’’

She swallowed. ‘‘I said all right. I’ll dump him.’’

He smiled.

‘‘In two weeks.’’

His smile twisted into a scowl. ‘‘What’s wrong with today? Or better yet, yesterday.’’

‘‘Because I need him. I may be the brains in our investigation, but he’s the brawn. Like you said, we don’t know who—or what—we’re up against. Give us two weeks to find enough evidence to clear your name before you do anything drastic.’’

‘‘No way.’’

‘‘Would you rather have me do this on my own?’’

‘‘I’d rather lock you in a closet until I’m safely in Mexico City.’’

‘‘I’ve recently learned how to pick locks, so that won’t do you any good. But I will make you a deal.’’

He narrowed his eyes. ‘‘What kind of deal?’’

‘‘I’ll dump Nick Chamberlin in two weeks if you’ll promise to stay put for that long.’’

‘‘Stay put?’’ he asked innocently.

‘‘You know what I mean. No midnight taco runs.’’

‘‘All right,’’ he agreed grudgingly. ‘‘It will take me that long to work all the details out anyway. But I don’t like the idea of you spending even one more day with this guy, much less two weeks. I’m going to make sure Weasel keeps an eye on you.’’

Just what she needed. Another man peeking through her windows. ‘‘That really isn’t necessary.’’

‘‘I think it is. No offense, Lucy, but you don’t know guys like I do. They’re not like those romantic heroes in your favorite novels.’’ He cleared his throat. ‘‘Men and women are made differently.’’

She bit back a smile. "I think we covered this about fifteen years ago. I distinctly remember the diagrams."

A blush stained Melvin's stubbly cheeks. "I'm not talking about physical differences. Men and women *think* differently. Now take Vanessa..."

"You take her," Lucy quipped. "Or better yet, let's give her to your ex-lawyer and show him the real meaning of cruel and unusual punishment."

"I know Vanessa is spoiled and vain and selfish, but she has her good points, too."

"Thanks to liposuction."

"Face it, Luce. Men are attracted to beautiful women. It's been that way forever. We're also attracted to not-so-beautiful women. And tall women. And short women. And skinny women. And—"

"I think I get your point," Lucy interjected. "If it's in a skirt, it's fair game."

"Exactly. And I don't like the idea of Chamberlin using you for target practice."

"I told you Nick isn't like that."

"*All* guys are like that. If they can't have a fantasy woman like Vanessa, then they'll take the next best thing."

"Gee, thanks."

"You know what I mean."

Unfortunately she did. Nick might be immune to her charms, but according to Melvin he would fall right into Vanessa's web—with his arms wide open.

"Men are such idiots," she murmured aloud.

"Now that's what I like to hear," he said. "Keep that thought whenever you're around Chamberlin during the next two weeks."

Lucy blinked. "Oh, right. Two weeks." For the first time she noticed the shadows under Melvin's eyes and the loose fit of his bright orange prison uniform. He'd lost weight.

For a brief moment she felt a pang of guilt for making him stay incarcerated even one more day. "Just two more weeks. Can you wait that long, Melvin?"

"Sure," he said with his familiar, cocky grin. "I'll put the time to good use. José and his invisible friend are giving me Spanish lessons."

NICK WALKED into the Westview police station on Monday afternoon. Surprisingly, it looked the same as it had that day eighteen months ago when he'd been escorted from the premises. Same pea-green walls. Same blinking telephones. Same leaky coffeepot. He sidestepped the coffee-soaked paper towels on the tile floor as he strode past a silent, staring trio of uniformed officers.

His face wasn't on any of the Ten Most Wanted posters, but he was greeted with the same looks of suspicion and disdain as public enemy number one. He really couldn't blame them. Nobody liked a dirty cop.

Nick walked past the reception desk to the tiny office he used to share with his partner. Cole looked the same, too, sitting in front of his computer monitor with a pencil clamped between his teeth. His tie hung loose around his neck, his dark hair was ruffled. He pecked at the keyboard with one finger, intent on his work.

"Still trying to learn the alphabet, I see," Nick said, stepping through the doorway.

"Nick!" Cole jumped out of his chair, slapping his old friend on the back. "Man, it's great to see you."

Despite Cole's laid-back attitude, his athleticism and quick instincts had made him invaluable on the streets. Even after Nick's arrest, Cole had never let him down. His long, humorous letters had gotten Nick through more than one sleepless night in prison.

"So what brings you here?" Cole asked, clearing a chair of haphazardly stacked file folders so Nick could sit down.

"I'm doing some investigative work."

Cole's dark brows shot up. "Really? That sounds right up your alley. You always were the smart one."

"If I was the smart one, what does that make you?"

Cole grinned. "The good-looking one."

Nick shook his head. "You haven't changed a bit, Rafferty."

"I'm betting neither have you. You're still the same decent, upstanding cop you were eighteen months ago. The one who pleaded guilty to a crime I know he didn't commit."

"Let's not get into that."

Cole perched on the corner of his desk. "Why not? I've been over it a hundred times. Your grandfather suffers a massive heart attack, you're driving his car to the hospital when you're pulled over for...what?"

"A routine traffic check."

"Right. And that's when they found all that marijuana stashed in the trunk of the car. The same marijuana missing from the evidence room at the station. But what really doesn't make sense is your confession. I *know* you'd never do something like that."

"I confessed, didn't I? I wasn't about to put my grandparents through a lengthy, messy investigation and trial. Not with everything else they were going through. Look, I paid the price. It's over and done with now. Let's just forget it."

"Can you do that, Nick? You lost everything."

"I'll do whatever I have to do."

Cole knew when to stop pushing. "So tell me about your case."

"Does the name Mad Dog Moore sound familiar?"

"Are you kidding? The guy's practically a legend around here. But he really blew it when he torched the Hanover Building. I thought he was smarter than that."

"So you're convinced he did it?"

"Positive. I was the lead investigator. It's an open-and-shut case."

"What about his alibi?"

Cole shook his head. "Weak. Very weak. You'd think a guy with Mad Dog's colorful past would be more creative."

"He claims he was driving around Westview when the fire started?"

Cole nodded. "Some passerby called in a report of smoke coming out of the windows. Mad Dog finally showed up after the fire department put out the blaze."

"I suppose nobody saw him between the time of the fire and when he arrived on the scene?"

"Not a soul." Cole picked up a paper clip off his desk, twirling it with his fingers. "So why all the questions? Don't tell me Mad Dog hired you?"

"Nope. His sister, Lucy. She thinks he's innocent."

Cole whistled. "Mad Dog has a sister? I'll bet she's something to see. Let me guess, she's got spiked purple hair, missing teeth and twice as many tattoos as her brother."

Nick bit back a smile. "Not exactly."

"Well, she must be nuts if she thinks Mad Dog is innocent. In his apartment we found traces of the gunpowder he used as an accelerant. And the place was full of combustibles—all kinds of paint and varnish cans from the remodeling." Cole threw the mangled paper clip into the trash can. "As far as a motive, it's the usual."

"Money?" Nick guessed.

Cole nodded. "He insured the place a few weeks earlier

with a replacement policy for almost twice the building's original purchase price. Mad Dog claimed it would be worth that much after the renovations, but they'd barely begun when the place got torched."

"Didn't he realize the insurance company would never pay the full amount of the policy?"

Cole shrugged. "Guess he wasn't thinking straight. He sure wasn't thinking when he torched that place. It's a textbook arson case, Nick. And the trail literally leads right to Mad Dog's front door."

Nick sighed. "That's what I keep trying to tell Lucy."

"And she's not buying it?"

"Nope. She's convinced someone else is to blame. She's determined to find the *real* arsonist."

Cole grinned. "So what's your plan?"

Nick stretched his long legs out in front of him. It felt good to be back here like this, discussing a case with his old partner. Almost like old times.

"First I'm going to check out Ralph Rooney. Then—"

"Wait a minute," Cole interjected, holding up one hand. "Ralph Rooney? *The* Ralph Rooney? The president of the Friends of Westview Association? The man who's planning to run for mayor in the next election?"

"I know," Nick replied. "It's a long shot. But the least I can do is check him out. I mean, she *is* paying me to investigate the case."

"And Rooney's your only lead?"

Nick cleared his throat. "Not exactly. After I check out Rooney, Lucy has *arranged* for me to...um...interview Vanessa Beaumont."

"You've interviewed suspects before. Why do I get the feeling there's more to this story?"

"Because the way she arranged it was by having Vanessa buy me at a bachelor auction. We have a date next Friday night.''

Cole laughed. ''I've *got* to meet this Lucy. Sounds like you have your hands full, Chamberlin.''

''You have no idea.'' Nick reached into his pocket, pulling out a plastic bag. ''By the way, I'd like to have this checked out.''

''What is it?''

''A matchbook.''

Cole looked at the smudged, tattered matchbook through the plastic. ''Where did you get it?''

''At the crime scene.''

''You're kidding. We turned that place upside down.''

''It was wedged under a floorboard. Lucy helped me find it.'' He decided not to go into details. ''Can you get the lab to check it for fingerprints?''

''Sure thing.'' Cole frowned. ''But it looks pretty fragile. I'm not sure how well it will hold up under testing.'' He squinted at the gold lettering barely visible through the charcoal smudges. ''Is there writing on it?''

Nick nodded. ''I checked it out with a magnifying glass. The only words I could make out were *old, Fort* and *Ann.*

''Old Fort Ann? What is that? The name of a bar?''

Nick shrugged. ''Who knows? This is probably a long shot anyway. I didn't even tell Lucy about it. I don't want to get her hopes up.''

Cole nodded. ''I'll let you know the report as soon as I get the lab results.'' He tossed the bag onto his desk. ''Hey, why don't you meet me at Bailey's Bar and Grill tonight after my shift is over? We'll grab a burger, a pitcher of beer, and watch the game on the big screen. It'll be like old times.''

''Sorry, I've got to work tonight. A stakeout at Rooney's place.''

"With your new boss?" Cole grinned. "Some things never change. The only thing that ever kept you from 'Monday Night Football' was a woman."

"I'll be on my own this time. And it's a good thing, too."

"Because Lucy Moore is scarier than her brother?"

"Nope," Nick countered. "Because it's a Monday."

LATER THAT EVENING, Nick hunkered down in the driver's seat of Sadie's '89 Buick and told himself it could be worse. He could be sweeping up fish nuggets off the floor at Farley's Fish Hut.

The car sat like a big yellow U-boat along a curb on Aspen Drive, in the ritziest neighborhood in Westview. If the homeowners' association had a rule against ex-cons scoping out the condos and gated estates, he was in big trouble. He could just imagine trying to explain all this to his parole officer. Somehow the excuse, "A librarian made me do it," sounded lame even to his ears.

But this particular librarian seemed able to make him do just about anything. It worried him, because he'd never been a pushover with women before. He'd always been the one calling the shots, whether it was with an investigation or a relationship. He wasn't domineering, just in control of his own life.

Except with Lucy.

So far, he'd broken into a building for her, put himself on the auction block for her, and now he was spying on rich people for her. He needed to figure out this power she had over him, before she got any more brilliant ideas.

Maybe it was her eyes. Soft, big brown eyes that could sparkle with mischief one moment and melt his defenses the next. Or her blond hair, as unmanageable as Lucy herself. Or that crooked smile of hers that niggled something way down deep in his gut. Then there was her body.

Even after fifteen months without a woman, he still had a discerning eye. Most men wouldn't look beyond those conservative clothes she wore at the library. But he had a great imagination. And he'd seen her in that blue dress. Seen her soft, enticing curves. The gentle sway of her hips. Those long, long legs.

He closed his eyes as he leaned back against the headrest. Thanks to his great imagination he could now see her *out* of that blue dress. Her skin warm and silky smooth. Her lips pink and slightly parted as she walked toward him. His gaze falling on those legs and that tempting mouth and everywhere in between.

His eyes snapped open and his head jerked up. He definitely didn't want to start having fantasies about Lucy, especially a *naked* Lucy. He looked around the front seat, desperate for something to distract him from his too-vivid imagination.

Picking up the flattened cardboard hat off the dashboard, he scowled at the colorful dancing cod. In the dim glow provided by the streetlight, he studied the directions on the inner panel. *Insert flap A into flap F. Tuck flap B under flap H. Fold flap D along the dotted line.* His fingers fumbled over each other as he tried to manipulate the small paper tabs. *Bend flap C over flap E.* Flap C? Nick turned the cardboard over in his hands. Where the hell was Flap C?

Maybe he wasn't ready for the French fry machine. He couldn't even put together a simple cardboard hat. But that meant staying with Lucy. How long could he continue taking money for a case that was already solved? He tossed the mangled hat into the back seat, wishing he could toss his conscience aside just as easily. Most people already thought he was without morals or ethics. So why not fulfill their expectations? He certainly didn't have anything more to lose.

Except possibly his sanity.

"Nick."

The eerie whisper startled him out of his reverie. He peered out the car windows but saw only the silhouette of looming willow trees and the soft glow of lights in the gated estate windows. As the wind rustled the tree leaves, he thought he heard the sound again.

"Nick."

The hairs prickled on the back of his neck. He'd never questioned his sanity before, but hearing voices wasn't a good sign. He knew if he started talking back he would really be in trouble. He began humming to drown out the disconcerting sound.

But he could still hear that husky voice calling to him.

"Nick," it rasped. "Ni...i...ck."

At that moment he chose to start singing the chorus to "Surrey with the Fringe on Top" while tapping his fingers in rhythm against the steering wheel.

A head suddenly appeared in the passenger window. Startled, his body jerked in reaction, his knee slamming against the steering column. "Ow!"

"Did you hurt yourself again?"

Lucy. He should have known. He reached over to unlock the passenger door, then popped it open. She was crouched in the grass, dressed entirely in black—from the knit cap concealing her blond hair to the black leotard that stretched over her slender body to the black leather boots on her feet.

"Who are you supposed to be?" he asked, as she climbed into the seat. "Catwoman?" Then another thought occurred to him as he warily eyed the bulging black knapsack slung over her shoulder. "Don't tell me we're crashing a masquerade party, because I'm putting my foot down, Lucy...."

She closed the car door, then looked at him, her brow crinkled above her brown eyes. "What are you talking about? We're on a stakeout. I just didn't want anyone to see me."

"Where did you come from? I didn't see any headlights."

"I parked around the corner and sort of moved from tree to tree until I reached the car."

"You're soaking wet," he observed, uncomfortably aware of the way the leotard clung to her body.

She pulled off the knit cap, her damp hair falling haphazardly out of its bun. "That's because you left me sitting out on the lawn until the automatic sprinklers came on!"

"I was singing," he muttered, as she slid the knapsack off her shoulder.

"I heard. You do have a great voice," she said. "And I love show tunes, especially from *Oklahoma.* Do you know the words to 'I Cain't Say No'?"

He knew it down to the dance steps, but he wasn't about to admit it. "What are you doing here?"

"I brought you something." She unzipped the knapsack.

"Valium?"

"Even better," she said, reaching inside. "I've got some great stuff here. Pretzels, peanuts, caramel corn, potato chips, chocolate bars, diet soda..."

"Diet soda?"

"I'm trying to watch my weight."

"Lucy," he began as she tossed him a beef jerky stick, "what's with all the junk food?"

She pulled a pretzel out of the bag. "To keep up our energy. It could be a long night."

"For me, maybe. But I work alone."

She shook her head. "Unwise. According to Leo Bronski, stakeouts require at least two people so the investigation isn't compromised. It's too easy to fall asleep or start daydreaming and miss something important when you're all by yourself."

He didn't mention the type of daydreams he'd been having before she showed up. Daydreams he couldn't quite forget while she was sitting next to him in that revealing leotard.

"Who is Leo Bronski?" he asked, popping open a can of diet soda.

"I can't believe you don't know," she said, munching on her pretzel. "His books, *Under the Gun* and *The Felony Files,* are national bestsellers."

Nick rolled his eyes. "Not more of those supercop books."

"He's a great writer," she said, rolling up the pretzel bag, "and a retired police detective. So all his stories are based on real-life experiences. They're fascinating. And he's been on hundreds of stakeouts."

"Lucy, this isn't some storybook fantasy," he said, finishing off his beef jerky. "In fact, it's actually a complete waste of time. We're not going to find out anything about Melvin's case here. Ralph Rooney is a prominent, respected businessman. He's even on the governor's crime-prevention panel."

"Which is why no one would ever suspect him. Did you know he made several offers to buy the Hanover Building before the fire, but Melvin refused to sell it to him?"

"So Rooney decides to torch the place? That just doesn't make sense."

"Well, somebody torched it."

"Lucy..."

"Duck!" She suddenly grabbed him by the shirtfront

and pushed him down lower in the seat. The back of his head bumped hard against the armrest on the door as his legs tangled with hers.

Nick reached up to rub his head. "What do you think you're doing?"

"Don't move," Lucy whispered, her lithe body stretched out on top of him, her hands gripping his shoulders. "I think someone is looking over here."

"Well, if he saw us, he's really going to be suspicious now."

She looked down at him. "Not if..." Her voice trailed off and he saw her swallow.

"Not if...what?"

Her fingers flexed on his shoulders. "Not if whoever is out there thinks we're just...parking."

"I've been parked here for the last thirty minutes."

She wrapped her arms around his neck. "That's not exactly what I mean."

He opened his mouth but Lucy's lips met his before he could say a word. His vivid imagination never even came close to the reality of Lucy in his arms. Her tentative, feather-light kiss. Her mouth moving over his, gentle and delving, luscious and lingering.

Nick's arms wrapped around her, his hands caressing the length of her back, warming her cool, moist leotard. Her body relaxed into his. Her mouth tasted salty and sweet. So sweet that he almost groaned aloud when she finally broke the kiss.

"Nick," she breathed heavily, her brown eyes wide and slightly dazed, her mouth still only scant inches from his.

The beam of a flashlight swept slowly past the windshield, now partially steamed over.

"He's still out there," Nick whispered raggedly.

She hovered above him, lightly brushing his hair with her fingertips. "Good."

She kissed him again, her tongue tentatively exploring his mouth. He moaned low in his throat, his hands moving to her hair. He pulled the bobby pins out and let his fingers luxuriate in the thick, damp curls that spilled over her shoulders. Every nerve ending in his body reacted as Lucy shifted atop him, deepening the kiss.

He wondered briefly what book taught her to kiss like this; then he stopped thinking at all. He only wanted to feel—feel her soft, pliant body molded against his own, her hands everywhere. He anchored one arm around her narrow waist and slowly turned them both on the wide seat until their positions were reversed. He'd never loved this big, roomy boat of a car more than he did at this moment.

She broke the kiss with a gasp of surprise as she now found him on top of her. "I don't think..." she began.

He silenced her with another kiss. A raw, sensual kiss filled with all the pent-up frustration and desire he'd felt ever since he first laid eyes on her. A kiss he never wanted to end.

The soft whimpers emanating from her throat thrilled him—at first. Then they made him hesitate. Were they whimpers of passion? Or protest? Maybe he'd been without a woman so long, he'd lost control. Maybe she was as terrified by his response as he was.

He lifted his head, his breathing as fast and shallow as hers, and stared into her wide brown eyes.

"Oh, Nick." He swallowed at the tremor in her voice. Darkness blanketed the fogged car windows. "He's gone. I think we fooled him."

"What?"

"The guy with the flashlight," she said, rising up on her elbows. "He must have believed we were really lovers."

She blinked up at him, the heat fading from her eyes. "You can get up now."

He didn't want to get up. He wanted to sink into her soft body and kiss her breathless. He wanted to explore every inch of her under that leotard. He wanted to hold on to Lucy and never let her go.

"I can't breathe," she said.

With a deep sigh, he reluctantly shifted his weight off her, his foot catching on the door handle and his elbow connecting solidly with the steering wheel. The sharp blare of the car horn covered his grunt of pain.

"So much for keeping a low profile," Lucy cried, struggling to get out from underneath him.

He emitted a stifled groan. "Watch your knee."

"Sorry," she murmured, pulling herself up to a sitting position. Then she frowned at the front windshield. "It's all steamed up in here. I can't see a thing."

The windows weren't the only thing steamed up. Nick tugged at his shirt collar. If only the automatic sprinklers would come on again so he could have the best alternative to a cold shower. He took several slow, deep breaths and tried not to think about Lucy. Or that hot, passionate kiss. Or that he really wanted to kiss her again. That he really wanted her.

He was starting to hyperventilate. If he didn't calm down, he'd get dizzy. Maybe he'd pass out. Maybe Lucy would have to give him mouth-to-mouth resuscitation.

This was really getting pathetic.

"I can't stand it anymore," she said, rolling down her fogged window.

That made two of them, Nick thought.

He turned to reach for her as a swift gust of brisk night air blew across the front seat. But it was the sound of a familiar masculine voice that chilled his hot blood.

"Hey, Luce. How come you never kissed me like that?"

5

"WEASEL," LUCY EXCLAIMED, brushing her tousled hair out of her eyes. "What are you doing here?"

"Wishing I'd taken you up on that marriage proposal." Weasel leaned in the open window, his arms resting on the door frame. "Or at least asked you out on a datc. I takc it you've changed your policy."

"Policy?" she echoed, still shaken by the impact of Nick's kiss. It scored at least a 9.5 on her own personal Richter scale.

"About not dating anybody with jail time—which pretty much excluded every guy on Bale Street," Weasel said with a good-natured shrug. "Mad Dog explained it to all of us one night after you'd turned down Snake. He said it was nothing personal, you just didn't want to get involved with a loser."

"I don't think I ever put it quite like that," she said, unable to deny it completely.

Nick sat silent and unmoving beside her. He could have been two hundred miles away from her instead of only two feet. He obviously didn't understand that she'd established that policy for a very good reason. She couldn't let anything, or more specifically, anyone interfere with her goals.

Her avid reading had taught her a lot, including how the main character in a novel always set a goal, then stopped at nothing to achieve it. Lucy had followed the same example in her life. In high school, her goal was to win a college scholarship. In college, her goal was to get her degree in library science. After accomplishing each goal, she set a new one, always determined to reach higher. And she'd never let love or lust get in her way. Until now.

Instead of pursuing her newest goal, which was fighting for her brother's freedom, she'd been making out in a parked car with an ex-con. Time to get her priorities straight.

"I made that policy for a reason," she explained.

Weasel nodded. "Hey, I understand. Why drag yourself down with a no-account bum when you're on the way up, when you've got such big dreams? Like a house in the Eagle Estates. The top job at the Heritage Library. A seat on the city council."

Her mouth fell open. "How do you know about that?"

"Me and Snake broke into your locker in high school and read your diary. Not too juicy, but you've got great penmanship."

She turned to Nick. "You can shoot him now."

"What exactly are you doing here," Nick growled, "besides spying on us?"

"I'm working as a valet. It's all part of the Protégé Project. Rooney hires me to park cars whenever he throws one of his ritzy dinner parties. He likes to bestow temporary employment on the underprivileged. It makes him feel special." Weasel's green eyes narrowed. "What exactly are *you* doing here, Chamberlin? Besides feeling up my best friend's sister."

His jaw clenched as Weasel's smirk widened. "Don't you have some cars to park?"

"I'd offer to park yours, but somehow I don't think you're here for the party."

"We're spying on Ralph Rooney," Lucy said. "Trying to find out if he has any connection to the fire."

"Oh." Weasel's smirk faded. "Gee, Luce, is there anything I can do?"

"Confess to the crime?" Nick suggested.

"No, thanks," Weasel said. "But I do have some information—" he paused, flicking an invisible piece of lint from his jacket "—if you're willing to deal."

"What kind of deal?" Nick asked.

"One hundred dollars or..."

"Or what?"

Weasel's gaze fastened on Lucy. "One kiss."

"You're not my type," Nick clipped.

"Good, because Lucy is definitely my type," Weasel said. "What do you say, Luce? Do we have a deal?"

Before she could even open her mouth, Nick tossed a wad of bills at Weasel. "Enough fooling around, Malone. What have you got?"

Weasel stuffed the bills in his shirt pocket with a disappointed sigh. "You don't know what you're missing, Lucy."

"Just tell us what you know," Nick growled.

"Okay. The night of the fire..."

"Yes," Lucy prompted, her heart beating faster.

"There was an eyewitness."

Nick snorted. "No kidding. Half the neighborhood turned out when the fire trucks showed up."

"No, I mean a real eyewitness. A person who saw somebody leave the Hanover Building around midnight. And *that* somebody wasn't Mad Dog."

Lucy's fingers clutched the armrest. "Then who was it?"

Weasel shrugged. "She didn't say."

"She?" Nick asked.

"One of the girls who works a corner downtown. I heard about her from a friend of a friend."

"A prostitute?" Lucy guessed.

"That's right. I think her name is Daisy. Or maybe Rose. Some flower name."

"You *think?*" Nick said. "I just paid you a hundred bucks. I expect some quality information for that price. How do we even know it's true? And why didn't she report this to the police?"

Weasel laughed. "The police? Yeah, right." He stepped back from the car, looking toward the house. "Looks like the party is starting to break up. I've got to get back to work."

"Thanks, Weasel," Lucy called as he strolled away. He'd just given them the biggest lead in the case. She could barely contain her excitement as she turned to Nick. "This is it! I can go undercover. She'll probably talk to me if she thinks I'm another hooker. And I've got the perfect dress...."

"No way."

"But Nick..."

"Forget it, Lucy. It's out of the question. In the first place, you could never pass as a hooker."

She wasn't sure if he meant that as an insult or a compliment. Either way, she hoped it wasn't true. She had to pass for a prostitute if she ever wanted to find Daisy, or Rose, or Magnolia.

"And in the second place," Nick continued, "it's much too dangerous down there at night. Believe me. I used to work that beat when I was a rookie. It's no place for a librarian."

Now *that* was an insult—and a challenge. One she fully intended to meet. She could pull it off, too. All she needed was a little time, some tenacity...and a Miracle Bra.

"I'M READY for a good, juicy murder."

Lucy hid a yawn behind one hand as she scribbled Sadie

Chamberlin's comment on her notepad. Ever since the stakeout three nights ago, she'd been up late researching every book available on the world's oldest profession. Now she could barely stay awake for the Merry Widows Book Club meeting. As discussion leader, it was her responsibility to provide good reading recommendations.

She looked around at the time-weathered faces of the club's five regular members: Sadie Chamberlin, Edith Cummings, Veda Tavlik, Lenora Eberly and Goldie Schwartz. They all had two things in common: dead husbands and a love of books.

"Any other suggestions?" Lucy asked, trying to focus her mind on fiction. Lately, real life had demanded all of her attention. She only had eight more days until Melvin attempted his prison break, and twenty-four more hours until she transformed herself from a librarian into a lady of the evening.

A tingle of anticipation shot through her. While Nick was on his date with Vanessa tomorrow evening in search of information, she'd be walking the streets in search of the eyewitness. Her costume was almost ready and she'd stocked up on hair spray just in case she encountered trouble.

"I want something challenging, like a complicated murder mystery," Edith said. Shortly after her retirement, Edith had qualified for the semifinals of the senior citizens' tournament on the "Jeopardy!" TV game show. She loved to read mysteries, solving most of them before the group got halfway through the book.

"Nick and Lucy are trying to solve a real mystery," Sadie announced. "Her brother is accused of arson and they're trying to find the real culprit."

"How fascinating!" Goldie exclaimed. At forty-eight, Goldie was the youngest member of the Merry Widows

Book Club. She qualified for membership after the death of her fourth husband, newspaper magnate Wilson Schwartz. Though now financially independent, she still wrote her popular gossip column for the *Westview Herald.*

"Frustrating is more like it," Lucy said with a sigh. "If we could just find the real arsonist, Melvin could be free. But we're running out of time, and the police are convinced he's guilty."

Veda, a sixty-eight-year-old grandmother who jogged three miles a day, leaned forward in her chair. "Are you saying your brother didn't start that fire, but someone else is letting him take the blame?"

Lucy nodded. "The real arsonist is feeling smug and safe while an innocent man goes to jail."

Edith brushed a speck of lint off her neatly pressed "Jeopardy!" T-shirt. "Just like Horace Dexter in that book, *Murder for Sale.* Remember, girls? We read it last summer."

Sadie nodded. "Horace killed the doctor, then framed that nice young lady. Nobody would have discovered the truth if the detective hadn't tricked him by planting that article in the newspaper."

Veda snapped her fingers. "That's right. The one that said he'd found the murder weapon and planned to have it tested for fingerprints."

For a moment no one said a word. Lucy tried to tell herself it could never work, but the more she thought about it, the more possible it seemed. "Do you think I should do it? Try to flush out the real arsonist by claiming there's new evidence that will break the case wide open?"

"Well, it certainly couldn't hurt," Sadie mused.

"I could put an item in my column," Goldie offered, her blue eyes gleaming with excitement. "Give a review of the case and then put in the plug about the new evidence. All with my trademark flair, of course."

Sadie clapped her hands together. "Then when the real arsonist reads it, he'll panic and possibly reveal himself."

"*If* he reads it," Veda said.

Goldie sniffed. "*Everybody* in Westview reads my column." Then she smiled at Lucy. "I'll make sure it gets in tomorrow's paper."

"Goldie, that would be wonderful," Lucy exclaimed, almost afraid to get her hopes up. "Thank you all so much. Now I've taken up enough time with my personal problems. We're here to talk about books."

Lenora, the group's oldest member at eighty-two, held up a thick volume in her hand. "I just finished *Out of the Blue.* It's got some nice gory parts in it, but it's a little light on the sex."

"I'm in the mood for another good love story," Veda Tavlik said, pulling knitting needles and a skein of baby blue yarn out of her tote bag, "like that one we read last month. It was really hot."

Sadie nodded. "Wasn't that Stone character a hunk?"

"He reminded me of your grandson," Goldie chimed.

"Nicky is quite good-looking," Veda added, clicking her knitting needles together, "with those big broad shoulders. He's certainly handsome enough to take a young girl's breath away. Don't you think so, Lucy?"

Lucy blinked, her mind still on the image of Nicky Chamberlin's broad, bare shoulders. "What?"

"Lucy and my grandson went on a date last week," Sadie confided to the group. "He got her the loveliest corsage."

Lenora's thin, blue-veined hand fluttered up to her chest. "Isn't that romantic? I think flowers are such a poetic way for a man to express his true feelings. My Henry always gave me bouquets of lavender.''

''What kind of flowers did Nicky give you?'' Edith asked.

''Roses,'' Lucy replied. ''Champagne roses.''

The women oohed and aahed until Lenora had to take a whiff from her oxygen tank.

''Roses can mean love,'' Goldie informed them.

''It was only our first date,'' Lucy said. ''And *I* asked *him* out.''

''But you do like him?'' Sadie asked.

Edith snorted. ''What's not to like? That grandson of yours is one handsome hunk of man, Sadie. If I were a few years younger, I'd set my cap on him myself.''

''I think you mean a few decades younger, Edith,'' Veda said with a smile. ''Besides, we don't want Lucy to have any competition. You are almost thirty, aren't you, dear?''

''In two years,'' Lucy admitted, wondering how the discussion had turned from hot books to her not-so-hot love life.

Lenora reached over and patted her hand. ''Don't worry, Lucy, you still have a little time left. Nicky is a fine man, and there comes a time when a woman can't be so choosy.''

''Why don't you come over to the house tomorrow evening?'' Sadie suggested. ''I'll fix a nice, romantic dinner for two, and then disappear.''

''Make oyster stew,'' Edith said. ''Oysters are an aphrodisiac.''

''The man's been in prison for over a year,'' Goldie reminded them. ''I hardly think he'll need any additional stimulation. One kiss and he'll be a goner.''

Lucy swallowed. The memory of Nick's kiss last Monday night still made her woozy. Or maybe it was lack of

PLAY...

"ROLL A DOUBLE!"

PEEL OFF LABEL AND PLACE INSIDE

GET 2 BOOKS

AND A

FABULOUS MYSTERY BONUS GIFT

ABSOLUTELY FREE!

SEE INSIDE...

NO RISK, NO OBLIGATION
TO BUY...NOW OR EVER!

1. Peel off label from front cover. Place it in space provided at right. With a coin, carefully scratch off the silver dice. Then check the claim chart to see what we have for you – TWO FREE BOOKS and a mystery gift – ALL YOURS! ALL FREE!

2. Send back this card and you'll receive brand-new Harlequin Love & Laughter™ novels. These books have a cover price of $3.50 each, but they are yours to keep absolutely free.

3. There's no catch. You're under no obligation to buy anything. We charge nothing – ZERO – for your first shipment. And you don't have to make any minimum number of purchases – not even one!

4. The fact is, thousands of readers enjoy receiving books by mail from the Harlequin Reader Service®. They like the convenience of home delivery...they like getting the best new novels BEFORE they're available in stores...and they love our discount prices!

5. We hope that after receiving your free books you'll want to remain a subscriber. But the choice is yours – to continue or cancel any time at all! So why not take us up on our invitation, with no risk of any kind. You'll be glad you did!

Terms and prices subject to change without notice.
©1990 Harlequin Enterprises Limited. ® and TM are trademarks owned by Harlequin Enterprises Ltd.

THIS MYSTERY BONUS GIFT COULD BE YOURS FREE WHEN YOU PLAY "ROLL A DOUBLE"

"ROLL A DOUBLE!"

SEE CLAIM CHART BELOW

102 HDL CJRH
(U-H-LL-11/98)

YES! I have placed my label from the front cover into the space provided above and scratched off the silver dice. Please send me all the gifts for which I qualify. I understand that I am under no obligation to purchase any books, as explained on the back and on the opposite page.

Name ______________________________
(PLEASE PRINT)

Address ______________________ Apt.# ________

City ______________ State ________ Zip ________

CLAIM CHART

2 FREE BOOKS PLUS MYSTERY BONUS GIFT

2 FREE BOOKS

1 FREE BOOK

CLAIM NO.37-829

All orders subject to approval. Offer limited to one per household.

PRINTED IN U.S.A.

The Harlequin Reader Service®— Here's how it works:

Accepting free books places you under no obligation to buy anything. You may keep the books and gift and return the shipping statement marked "cancel." If you do not cancel, about a month later we'll send you 4 additional novels and bill you just $2.90 each, plus 25¢ delivery per book and applicable sales tax, if any.* That's the complete price — and compared to cover prices of $3.50 each — quite a bargain! You may cancel at any time, but if you choose to continue, every other month we'll send you 4 more books, which you may either purchase at the discount price...or return to us and cancel your subscription.

*Terms and prices subject to change without notice. Sales tax applicable in N.Y.

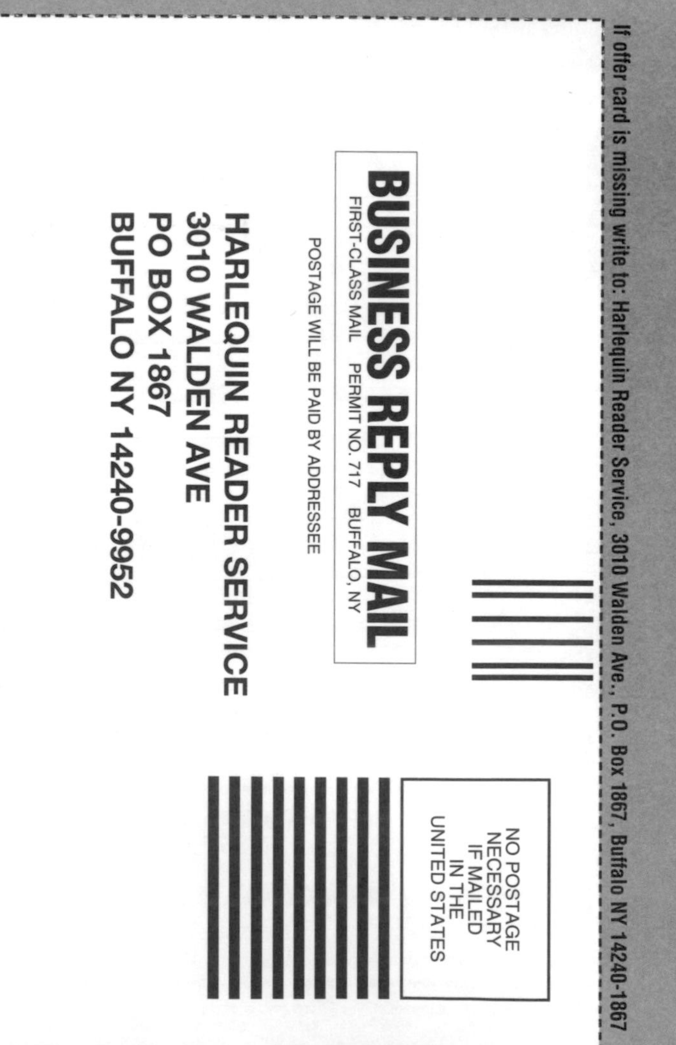

sleep. She didn't have enough experience with men to know if kisses usually caused such a strong physical reaction.

"You're right, Goldie," Veda said, counting the stitches on her knitting needle. "It will be almost too easy."

"Like shooting fish in a barrel," Lenora piped up.

Sadie clapped her hands together. "Then it's all set. Dinner for two at my house tomorrow night. Eight o'clock. Nicky will be thrilled."

Lucy couldn't keep silent any longer. "We'll have to do it another time. Nick will be at the Château Pierre tomorrow night...with Vanessa Beaumont." Five pairs of bifocals turned in her direction.

"On a date?" Edith asked.

"With whom?" Sadie asked in a weak voice.

"Vanessa Beaumont." Lucy twisted the ballpoint pen in her fingers. "She and Nick are having dinner together. It was...sort of my idea."

"Lucy, dear," Goldie said gently. "Men have such short attention spans. It's not a good idea to distract them by throwing other women in their paths."

Edith arched one silver brow. "Especially a woman like Vanessa."

Lucy wondered if she could possibly steer the conversation toward bunions again, an earlier topic of the evening. "It's not like that. Nick isn't romantically interested in her." She saw Veda and Goldie exchange glances. "Really. Vanessa may have information about the fire. That's the reason for the date. The only reason."

"So Nicky is sacrificing himself for you," Veda said. "Isn't that sweet?"

Lucy didn't know any man who would consider dating Vanessa a sacrifice. And what if the women were right?

What if Nick was vulnerable? Lonely? An easy victim to Vanessa's obvious charms?

She closed her eyes, telling herself it didn't matter. Telling herself as long as Nick kept his focus on the case, his private life was his own affair. Telling herself she didn't care what tactics Nick used to make Vanessa talk.

As long as he didn't touch her. Or order anything with oysters.

"I CAN'T BELIEVE you're here." Nick stood alone in the foyer of Château Pierre the next evening, glaring at the potted palm in the dimly lit corner. The palm fronds rustled suspiciously as he took a step closer.

He'd been on edge all week, wondering how Lucy would infiltrate herself into this phase of the investigation. He could hardly bring her along on his date, but hiding in the foliage seemed a little desperate, even for Lucy.

"I can't do my job if I have to keep looking over my shoulder, waiting for you to interfere. I am a former police detective. I can handle this investigation all by myself."

No response from the potted palm. He wondered briefly if Lucy knew how she affected him, how she drove him to do things a normal, thirty-three-year-old man shouldn't do. Like make out in a car. Or fantasize about a librarian. Or argue with a plant.

She also made it impossible for him to remain distant and cynical and hopeless. Because when she'd thrown herself on top of him in that car, he'd started hoping all kinds of things—things he'd soon learned could never come true. Because Lucy had a policy against men like him. And as soon as she accepted her brother's guilt and gave up on this case, she'd be out of his life. Forever.

"Don't you feel just a little bit ridiculous?" he asked, glimpsing a flash of blue between the leaves.

The maître d' approached, clearing his throat. "Excuse me, sir," he said, his gaze moving warily between Nick and the plant. "My name is Jacques. Is there a problem here?"

"Nothing I can't handle."

"Perhaps I can be of some assistance?"

Nick shook his head. "This is a private conversation."

Jacques moved back a step. "I see. Well, then perhaps it would be best to seat you now. We have a very attractive fern next to a private table in the back."

"My party hasn't arrived yet."

The maître d' glanced at the plant. "Do you have a reservation?"

He had plenty of reservations. This so-called date with Vanessa Beaumont was not only a dead end, but a potential disaster—especially with Lucy around. She was too unpredictable, too impulsive, too dangerous.

Hadn't he been punished enough in the last fifteen months?

He scowled at the potted palm as he reached into his jacket, pulling out the appointment card he'd received from the Friends of Westview Association. "Reservations for two at Château Pierre," he said, handing the card to Jacques.

"Ah. The Beaumont party. One moment, please." Jacques moved back to his station.

Nick's gaze fell on a newspaper lying open on a mahogany pedestal table. He picked it up, a name highlighted in the Goldie's Nuggets gossip column catching his eye. His jaw dropped as he scanned the column.

Goldie foresees sparks between a certain Westview librarian named *Lucy* and a former police detective who can still heat up an investigation. They're working together to solve the case of the Hanover Building fire. While the courts want to lock up a certain *Mad Dog* in a cage for the crime, this hot twosome is on the trail of the real smoking bandit. And they've got sizzling new evidence that could blow the case wide open just in the *Nick* of time. Stay tuned for *Moore* details of this smoldering story....

Nick couldn't believe it. He blinked and read the column again. Not only did the item link him and Lucy romantically, it claimed new evidence that just didn't exist. Where would Goldie Schwartz come up with such a ridiculous story? There could only be one answer.

He turned back to the potted palm. "This time you've gone too far."

Jacques approached, clearing his throat. "Pardon me again, sir. Miss Beaumont has already arrived. If you'll just follow me...."

With one last warning glance at the quivering palm fronds, Nick stepped after the maître d'.

Lucy's description of Vanessa hadn't prepared him for the woman seated at the small, secluded table. He'd been too stunned by the bachelor auction to notice the top bidder. Although looking at her now, he wondered how he ever could have missed her.

Vanessa Beaumont was blatantly beautiful.

Sleek, dark hair framed a heart-shaped face. Deep green eyes gleamed beneath thick, lush lashes. A small, upturned nose and pouty, pink lips completed the picture of a breathtaking woman.

She smiled up at him, her face ethereal in the glow of the candlelight. "Hello there."

"Miss Beaumont," he said, seating himself across from her.

"I simply won't be satisfied unless you call me Vanessa," she said, running one finger around the rim of her wineglass. "And for two thousand dollars, I certainly expect plenty of satisfaction."

Great. His status had fallen all the way from respected cop to paid gigolo. Just how far did Lucy expect him to go to obtain information? He picked up his wineglass, swallowing the Burgundy in one long gulp.

"I took the liberty of ordering for us," Vanessa said. "The cuisine here is excellent. We'll start off with Champagne Oysters followed by Turtle Soup."

"Fine," he said,

Vanessa leaned forward. "Then, for the main course, Roast Capon in Peanut Sauce. How does that sound?"

"Itchy," he muttered.

"What?"

He reached for the wine bottle to refill his glass. Maybe he should just relax and enjoy the inevitable. Vanessa Beaumont seemed designed to make a man forget about his troubles. "I was just wondering what's for dessert?"

"Anything you'd like, Nick," Vanessa murmured, "anything at all." Then he felt her foot crawling up his pant leg.

The wine toppled over the top of the glass, spilling onto the white linen tablecloth and dripping down onto his suit.

He bolted out of his chair, wiping his pants with his napkin. "Excuse me for a moment." With a polite nod, he headed toward the sanctity of the men's room. He needed some solitude, some time to regroup—an escape plan.

Once inside, he took off his jacket, tossing it onto a chair. Then he bent over the sink, splashing cold water on his face. He straightened and mopped his face dry with a paper towel.

The reflection he saw in the mirror made him gasp out

loud. A woman with big red hair winked at him with her thick, false eyelashes. For a moment he panicked, thinking he'd entered the ladies' room by mistake.

"You missed a spot," said a familiar voice.

Lucy. Slowly turning around, it took a moment to register the fact that this woman with the big hair and the even bigger chest was his librarian. But it was definitely Lucy. He glimpsed a skimpy red dress beneath the long, brown trench coat. He took a deep breath. "This is the men's room."

"I figured that out already," she said. "The urinals gave it away." She took the paper towel out of his hand and reached up to dab at his damp temple.

"I can't believe you followed me in here, especially after what I told you in the foyer."

She blinked. "Foyer? I wasn't in the foyer."

He folded his arms across his chest. "Don't give me that innocent act. You were hiding behind the potted palm. I saw the leaves moving."

"It must have been a draft, because I've been waiting in here for the last twenty minutes." She shook her head. "It was a real eye-opening experience. You wouldn't *believe* how many men don't wash their hands."

He swallowed. "You mean, I was talking to a plant the entire time?"

"I guess so," she said. "But don't feel bad. You're supposed to talk to plants. It helps them grow."

"Except I kept expecting the plant to talk back to me." He shook his head. "No wonder the maître d' was looking at me like I was nuts."

"Why would you think I'd be hiding behind a plant? I'd never do anything that dumb."

"Gee, I don't know, Lucy. Why would you put peanut

butter on a bee sting? Why would you attack me with hair spray? Why would you show up in the men's room?"

"Because we need to map out our strategy. Now, I don't have much time...."

"Our strategy?"

She nodded. "This is the perfect opportunity to catch Vanessa off guard. Wine and dine her. Then go in for the kill."

"Excuse me?" Nick was still trying to find the real Lucy under that atrocious wig and all that makeup. Did she really think she could fool anyone with this ridiculous disguise?

"I want you to leave," he said. "Leave the men's room. Leave the restaurant. Leave me alone."

"I will," she said, then noticed the skeptical expression on his face. "I promise. I have plans tonight, too. But first I want to give you something."

He backed up a step as she reached into the pocket of the trench coat. She pulled out a small sheet of paper.

"I made up a series of questions. Try to work them into the conversation."

He looked down at the list. "You've got to be kidding."

"You can do it," she said. "Just use your imagination."

"I can just hear it now." He cleared his throat. "Vanessa, I'm on fire for you. And speaking of fires, did you happen to burn down Mad Dog's building?"

Lucy frowned at him.

"Or how about this," he continued. "Vanessa, you are the most beautiful woman on earth. Please say you'll be mine. Confess your love and your participation in the crime that took place on April nineteenth."

He shook his head. "Not only would it never work, it's a complete waste of time. We shouldn't be focusing the investigation on Vanessa."

"Why not?"

"Because she isn't the most logical suspect."

"If you're going to tell me she's too beautiful to be guilty..." Lucy began.

"No," he replied, dabbing at the wine spots on his jacket. "I mean, obviously she's a beautiful woman. Exquisite, really, if you like..."

"Please get to the point," Lucy interjected. "If Vanessa isn't guilty, then who is?"

"Weasel."

Her mouth dropped open. "Weasel? My Weasel?"

"How many other Weasels do you know?"

"That's ridiculous," she sputtered. "I've known him since he was eight years old. He used to practically live at our house. He might be a little rough around the edges, but he's actually very sensitive. Besides, he's Melvin's best friend. He'd never do anything to hurt him."

"Then why was he in the warehouse the night we broke in?"

"He told us..." Lucy sputtered to a stop.

Nick shrugged into his jacket. "You see. He never gave us a reason. And the police showed up before I could get any answers out of him."

"He had a key."

"He *said* he had a key. We never saw it."

"But that doesn't mean anything. If he didn't have a key, he could have been in there for a good reason."

"Like returning to the scene of the crime?"

She scowled at him. "You told me that never happens."

"It *rarely* happens. But Weasel doesn't exactly strike me as the most brilliant criminal mind. Maybe he was in the warehouse that night to recover evidence that might prove him guilty."

"And this is what you're basing your suspicions on?"

"No. I'm basing them on the fact that in 1982, Walter

'Weasel' Malone was arrested and charged with two counts of second-degree arson. His lawyer later got him off on a technicality."

"1982?" Lucy said. "But that would only make him...fourteen years old at the time."

"Maybe he was in training."

Lucy folded her arms around her inflated chest. "Look, Weasel's had a rough life growing up with a single mother in a houseful of kids. He's made a few mistakes along the way, but anybody who leaves dog food out in the alley for all the stray mutts can't be that bad. You're just saying all this because you don't like him."

"Maybe you're just intent on accusing Vanessa because you don't like her," Nick countered. "She could be an innocent victim in all of this."

Lucy rolled her eyes. "*Innocent* is not the word to describe Vanessa."

"Oh, that reminds me..." Nick said, thoroughly enjoying himself. It was nice to see someone else confused and frustrated for a change. "How far do you want me to go?"

"Go where?"

He straightened his tie. "With Vanessa. I mean, it's fairly obvious she's attracted to me. I suppose I'd be willing to sacrifice myself in the line of duty...."

"You are totally disgusting."

A toilet flushed. Lucy ducked behind the heavy fabric draped over the long French windows, the toes of her spiked red heels peeking out underneath.

Jacques emerged from one of the stalls. He eyed Nick, then looked furtively around the posh rest room, his gaze finally falling on the potted philodendron suspended from the ceiling. "I thought I heard a woman talking."

Nick pressed his lips together. The last thing he needed

was to try and explain Lucy's antics to the management of the Château Pierre. "There's nobody in here but me."

"So I see." The maître d' glanced at the philodendron again. "Pardon me for interrupting, sir," he whispered, quickly washing his hands before ducking out the door.

"That was a close one," Lucy said, emerging from below the drapery.

"Forget about him. And forget about Vanessa. I can handle her."

She arched one heavily penciled brow. "That's what I'm afraid of. You'll be drooling over her before they even serve the second course, and you'll blow a great opportunity."

"Give me a little credit," Nick said. "I've got great willpower. I probably won't start drooling until the fourth course."

"I didn't know you had a sense of humor," she said, looking completely unamused.

"No extra charge," he quipped, saluting her as he walked out the door.

6

NICK GLANCED at his watch as Vanessa droned on about her favorite subject: herself. He wasn't in any danger of drooling by the fourth course, but falling asleep was a definite possibility.

"And then I wrote a poem about my traumatic experience in the Miss Ohio Beauty Pageant," she said, retrieving a package of cigarettes from her beaded handbag.

"Bad hair day?" Nick ventured.

"Actually my hair looked absolutely fabulous." She fluffed her thick mane over her shoulders. "My hairdresser Raoul used a special avocado herbal shampoo blend with just a hint of real organic lemon juice. The lemon is supposed to bring out my hair's natural highlights."

"You were telling me about your traumatic experience," he prodded before she could begin another dissertation on blow-drying.

"Oh, right. The interview question."

She shuddered slightly, drawing a long, slim cigarette out of the pack. "It still haunts me."

"A tough one?"

"It was a trick question. The emcee asked me how the United States could solve the problem of illegal aliens."

"And what did you say?"

"That the United States is the greatest country on the planet and we shouldn't let any UFO's land here without permission."

Nick opened his mouth, then closed it again.

"Who knew he was talking about invading *foreigners?*" She sighed. "I lost a crown, the judges voted nay, when the emcee stumped me that day.... That's how my poem starts. My writer friend, Niles, just thought it was so powerful. He said reading it was physically painful for him."

"I can imagine."

She held up her cigarette. "Do you have a light?"

"Sorry, I don't smoke."

She fumbled around in her purse. "I should have a lighter in here somewhere... Ah, this will do." She pulled out a white matchbook with shiny gold lettering on the front. It looked disturbingly familiar.

"Allow me," he said, taking the matchbook out of her hand. The first line on the cover read Harold & Letitia, followed by Happy Fortieth Anniversary. It was a lot cleaner, but otherwise identical to the one he'd found in the warehouse. All the letters fit, too. Old in Harold, Fort in Fortieth, and Ann in Anniversary.

"Who are Harold and Letitia?" he asked, as he struck a match, then held the flame up to the tip of her cigarette.

"Mommy and Daddy." She took a deep drag, moaning softly with appreciation. "They had a big bash last April for their anniversary."

Nick slowly flipped the matchbook back and forth between his fingers. "When in April?"

She blew a stream of smoke into the air. "The nineteenth."

Nick felt a suspicious gnawing in the pit of his stomach. *April nineteenth.* The same night as the fire. "Personalized matchbooks. Must have been quite a party."

She shrugged. "It was a total bore for me. I'd just had a big fight with my boyfriend. But, of course, as hostess, I had to stay until the party ended. There's nothing quite like watching a group of tipsy senior citizens dancing the conga at two o'clock in the morning."

"And they gave away these at the party?" he asked, holding up the matchbook.

She rolled her eyes. "Dozens of them."

"Can I have this one?"

She shrugged her bony shoulders. "Sure. We've got a ton left over at home."

"Thanks," he said, pocketing the matchbook. "So, what kind of man would let his girlfriend dance the night away without him?"

Vanessa sighed. "Mad Dog threw an absolute fit when I forbade him to go to the party with me. But what could I do? He was a real cool guy, but naturally he just wouldn't fit in with Mommy and Daddy's crowd."

"Naturally," Nick agreed with a sardonic twist of his lips. *What did Mad Dog Moore ever see in this woman?*

"Who knew he'd go berserk and try to burn down his own building?"

"Maybe he didn't do it."

Vanessa took another drag on her cigarette. "That's what he claimed afterward. But he was obviously throwing a temper tantrum that night. He wouldn't even answer his phone when I called."

"What?"

"I called him around eleven-thirty," Vanessa said, "to see if he was through pouting. But he didn't pick up."

According to the police reports the fire had started shortly before midnight. Was it possible Mad Dog's alibi really was true? "Did you tell the police this?"

She shrugged. "I don't remember. They asked me all sorts of questions. But then they found all that gunpowder that started the fire, so we all knew Mad Dog did it."

Nick had barely digested this new twist in the case when

Jacques approached the table carrying a cordless telephone receiver. "Excuse me. You have a phone call, Mr. Chamberlin."

Surprised, Nick took the phone. With a polite nod, Jacques returned to his post.

"Hello?" Nick said, cradling the phone on his shoulder.

"Hi, Nick. It's me, Lucy. Pretend you don't know me."

"Believe me, I've tried." He glanced at Vanessa, who was dipping her spoon into the turtle soup.

"Is Vanessa still there?"

"Yes."

"Has she spilled anything yet."

"Just a little cleavage." Static crackled over the line. Then Nick thought he heard the sound of screeching tires. "Where are you?"

"I'm doing a little undercover work."

He didn't like the sound of that, or the ferocious gnawing in the pit of his stomach.

More static. "Oops. Someone's coming," Lucy said, her voice sounding far way. "Gotta go."

"Hey, wait a minute...." he began, but all he heard was the sound of a dial tone in his ear. Nick frowned at the phone in his hand before placing it on the table. Lucy obviously wasn't in the men's room anymore. But where the hell was she?

Vanessa looked up from her soup, her perfect brow wrinkled with annoyance. "Important call?"

Nick shook his head. "My librarian. She has something she wants me to check out."

The phone chirped. Once. Twice.

Nick reached for it, but Vanessa got to it first. She pushed the power button off. "You're all mine tonight, Nick, and I'm not a woman who likes to share. Now where were we?"

"About to move on to the next course," he said, more than ready to end this date. Especially since he had a new lead and a librarian to pursue. He picked up the dessert menu, pretending to study the choices while he tried to figure how to make a graceful exit. Vanessa might be visually stunning and every man's fantasy on the outside, but she certainly wasn't his fantasy woman. She wasn't warm. She wasn't kind. She wasn't...Lucy.

Of course Lucy wasn't exactly Lucy tonight either, dressed up like a three-dollar hooker. If he didn't know better...

A three-dollar hooker. Nick set the menu on the table as the realization washed over him. That costume she had on earlier obviously meant she intended to go undercover as a prostitute to catch this supposed eyewitness. He was torn between outrage and resignation. Maybe he should just let her play out this ridiculous charade. Let her stand on that street corner...in that skimpy red dress...in one of the worst sections of Westview...alone.

He stood up, tossing his napkin beside his plate. "It's been great, but I've got to go."

Vanessa looked at him in surprise. "Go? You can't just go. You're bought and paid for. You're all mine tonight, Nick."

"Maybe the Friends of Westview will give you a refund," he said as he placed a generous tip on the table.

Vanessa was still sputtering as he strode out the door of Château Pierre. Part of him felt like a heel for deserting her in the middle of their date, but he didn't have any choice.

Lucy was in big trouble. Again.

LUCY CLUTCHED her big handbag against her chest as she huddled against the cold brick wall of the Hanover Building. Somehow, going undercover as a prostitute wasn't quite as adventurous as she'd imagined. Teetering on her spiked heels, she looked up and down the shadowed street. So far, she'd gotten three leg cramps, two blisters and a run in her nylons—but no inside information from the regulars that walked the streets of downtown Westview.

She'd expected the women to either ignore her or laugh at her, but not to compete with her. Every time a prospective customer approached, one of the regular girls would sidle over so he could do some comparison shopping. Not that Lucy wanted to sell her body—for any price. Which was a good thing, because no one was buying.

And she was really trying not to take it personally.

At least her efforts weren't completely wasted. She'd handed out several bookmarks with the library's address and hours to the women on her corner, recommended books on everything from beauty tips to auto repair, even invited those who were interested to a library seminar on job training.

Lester wouldn't be happy, but then Lester was a bit of a snob. Every time she suggested implementing a literacy program for the underprivileged or inviting inner-city kids to the weekly story hour, he'd look at her as if she'd proposed an orgy. Of course, he'd led a sheltered life. At forty-seven, he still lived with his mother and spent most of his spare time with his collection of cheeses from around the world. Still, she got tired of his constant toadying to the wishes of Mrs. Beaumont and the other members of the Heritage Library Foundation. As library director, Lester needed to remember that the public library belonged to *all* the citizens of Westview.

Lucy stifled a yawn as she glanced at her watch. Fifteen more minutes, then she'd head for home. Maybe she'd try it again tomorrow night.

A pair of headlights shone in the distance. Lucy's fingers

curled around her handbag. A light blue Ford Escort had tailed her all the way to the Château Pierre restaurant earlier this evening, the same Ford Escort she'd been seeing in her rearview mirror for the past several weeks. But it had never been quite close enough for her to identify the driver.

The car passed under a streetlight, illuminating the shiny silver exterior. She let out her pent-up breath. It wasn't the same one. Probably just another oversexed seventeen-year-old with twenty dollars to burn. She'd given the last one a lecture on the dangers of sexually transmitted diseases and sent him on his way.

The car slowed as it approached her, the driver anonymous behind the shaded windows. Then it stopped, the whir of the electric window blending with the sounds of the street.

"Get in the car."

Lucy peered through the passenger window. "Nick, is that you? Where did you get the car?"

"Just get in, Lucy."

"You didn't steal it, did you?"

He closed his eyes. "Sadie's car is in the shop. This is a loaner. Now get in the car."

"How did you find me?" Lucy edged closer. "And what happened to Vanessa?"

"We aren't going to discuss this now," he said, his voice strained. "Get in the car."

"I'm fine. Really. There was a little mishap between some rival gang members earlier, but it's pretty quiet now." Lucy waved him on. "You're going to blow my cover. I'll call you in the morning. We'll compare notes."

He dropped his head forward, banging it lightly against the steering wheel.

She walked to the curb, leaning into the open window. "Are you all right?"

He sighed as he lifted his head. "I think I'm having a nervous breakdown."

"Well, don't have it here! I'm trying to flush out a witness—the woman who might be able to identify the real arsonist."

"In that outfit, you'll flush out every pervert in Westview! Now, are you going to get in this car, or do I have to come after you?"

She tugged up the low neckline of her costume, a red sequin cocktail dress she'd bought for a New Year's Eve party ten years ago, but which was now two sizes too small. "I'm trying to blend in."

He shook his head in disbelief. "Don't you realize how dangerous it is out here?"

"Don't worry about me," she said. "I've got plenty of hair spray and great instincts. Besides, I grew up in the meanest neighborhood in Westview. I can take care of myself."

Nick got out of the car, circling the front bumper to stand beside her on the sidewalk. "We are not going to argue about this anymore." He grabbed her elbow. "Now let's go."

A voluptuous bleached blonde appeared out of the darkness. Her neon pink hot pants clashed with the orange halter top that stretched across her ample chest.

"What's your hurry, darlin'?" she asked, snapping her bubble gum. "How 'bout letting Babette join the party?"

Lucy whirled out of Nick's grasp and extended her hand to the prostitute. "Good evening, Babette. I'm Lucy. Have you been working this neighborhood long?"

Babette's gaze moved from Nick to the shiny Buick Century. "Long enough to know a big spender when I see one."

Nick folded his arms across his chest. "We're looking

for a woman named Daisy, or Chrysanthemum, or...some flower name. Do you know her?"

Babette ran one long fingernail down the length of his coat sleeve. "Honey, you don't need to look any farther. I'm your woman. You want something from Babette, you just have to ask."

"And pay," Nick said dryly.

Babette shrugged. "Business is business, darlin'."

"That's what I thought." He grasped Lucy's elbow. "Let's go."

Lucy didn't budge. Her instincts told her Babette knew something. She looked up at Nick. "No, not yet. She might really be able to help us."

"Lucy..."

She squeezed his arm. "Please."

With a reluctant sigh, Nick took out his wallet and withdrew a twenty-dollar bill. He handed it to Babette. "Now what do you have to say that's so important?"

Babette tucked the bill inside her generous cleavage, then drew out a shiny silver badge. "You're under arrest, darlin'."

"YOU'RE OFF THE HOOK, Chamberlin," Cole Rafferty said as he strode into his tiny office at the Westview police station, "thanks to your friend Lucy."

"Lucy is the one who got me into this mess in the first place," Nick muttered, raking his fingers through his hair. "She's impossible."

Cole grinned. "At last, a woman who can put a few dents in the Chamberlin armor. Sounds like a keeper."

Nick scowled at his old friend. "Very funny. Keep it up, Rafferty, and I'll have her demonstrate some of her self-defense techniques. You'll never be the same again."

"Actually, I might take you up on the offer. I've always been partial to big brown eyes."

"Stay away from her," Nick barked. Then his tone softened. "She's a dangerous woman."

Cole laughed out loud. "Dangerous? That sweet librarian, who must be all of five foot three? Give me a break, Nick. Just tell me she's off-limits and I'll keep my distance."

"She's off-limits."

Cole tipped back in his chair, clasping his hands behind his head. "So my old partner has finally taken the fall. Was it love at first sight?"

Nick frowned. "More like hives at first sight. Love has nothing to do with me and Lucy. She hired me to do some investigative work. That's it."

Cole smiled. "Right."

"If you don't believe me, just ask her."

"I did. She told me your relationship is strictly professional," Cole said. "And that Babette misunderstood your little transaction."

"Babette." Nick shook his head. "Is that really her name?"

"Yep. The department's newest recruit. A good cop, but a little overzealous in her work."

"Overzealous?" Nick echoed, rolling one stiff shoulder. "That woman put me in an headlock so fast, I could hear bones cracking. Where did you find her? 'American Gladiators'?"

"Hey, we had to fill the void somehow after we lost you."

A terse silence filled the room.

"Ready to tell me what really happened eighteen months ago?" Cole asked.

"That case is closed," Nick said evenly. "I'd rather talk

about the case against Mad Dog. Did you find any fingerprints on that matchbook I gave you?''

Cole shook his head. ''Nope. And it pretty much disintegrated during the testing. So I guess you're at a dead end.''

''Maybe not.''

That got Cole's attention. He leaned forward, resting his elbows on top of the scratched desktop. ''You've got a new lead?''

''I'm working on it.'' Nick fingered the new matchbook in his pocket. ''Could you do me a favor?''

''Name it.''

''Harold and Letitia Beaumont held an anniversary party the same night as the fire. I'd like to see a guest list.''

''I'll see what I can do.'' Then Cole's brow furrowed. ''Are these Beaumonts related to Mad Dog's old girlfriend?''

Nick nodded. ''Her parents. But Mad Dog wasn't invited to the party. He and Vanessa had a big blowup about it.''

''That's right.'' Cole rubbed his chin. ''Actually, that plays into his motive. He wanted to impress his rich girlfriend, so he set fire to the warehouse for the insurance money.''

''Lucy thinks he's innocent.''

Cole grinned. ''So she's pretty, sexy *and* loyal. A lethal combination. No wonder you're a lost cause. Does she have a sister?''

''As I said before, you haven't changed a bit, Rafferty.''

''Hey, somebody has to ask the tough questions. Why don't you and Lucy join me for a beer after my shift is over? I can tell her about the time you commandeered a hang glider to pursue a suspect.''

''No way. Those days are over for me. I'm playing it safe now. And I certainly don't need Lucy to get any more crazy ideas. After this last stunt, I'm tempted to lock her inside her apartment and throw away the key."

"You don't approve of her undercover work?"

Nick stood up and began pacing back and forth across the office. "Approve of her masquerading as a prostitute in one of the most crime-ridden sections of Westview? No I don't approve. She could have been assaulted... nabbed...killed." He swallowed hard. "I don't even want to think about it."

"You want to tell me again how she doesn't mean anything to you?"

"It's not like that," he explained, trying to understand these odd feelings himself. "I just feel responsible for her. She's alone, vulnerable and..."

"Dangerous?"

Nick stopped and let out a deep breath. "Extremely."

Cole nodded. "I think you may be right, Nick. Lucy Moore may just be the most dangerous woman you've ever met."

LUCY COULD SENSE a lecture coming on, and she just wasn't in the mood. A full moon glowed in the night sky. A lilting ballad played softly on the car radio as Nick pulled up along the curb in front of her apartment building. The roomy front seat of the loaner car reminded her of another car...another front seat...another night alone in the moonlight with Nick. And a kiss she couldn't seem to forget.

She swallowed a sigh, fingering the bright red curls of the wig on her lap. She'd scrubbed off all her makeup at the police station and pinned her gaping bodice shut with the safety pin Nick had thrust at her. He'd barely said two words to her since the arrest, but she could see his jaw working and knew he couldn't contain himself much longer. She settled back against the seat, waiting for the lecture to begin.

"Let's go," he snapped, switching off the ignition.

She blinked. "Where?"

Nick turned to look at her. "Up to your apartment. We have some things to discuss."

She didn't like the sound of that. And she definitely didn't want him to see her apartment in its current condition.

"Come on, Lucy," he prodded. "I've wasted enough time tonight already."

"My place is a mess."

"I won't even notice." He popped the door open and stepped out of the car before she could say another word.

For an employee, he wasn't very good at taking orders.

Lucy dragged herself behind him, all too aware of his loose-hipped stride and the wide breadth of his shoulders. She forced herself to look away. Melvin was running out of time, she was running out of money and Nick was running out of patience. The last thing she needed to do was fantasize about the hired help.

She had to keep her head, because no matter how good he looked in his clothes—or how much better he might look out of them—she still had to face facts. Nick Chamberlin was an ex-con. A dirty cop. A thirty-three-year-old man who lived with his grandmother.

But he was also a great kisser.

Unfortunately, that probably wasn't enough to base a relationship on. Not that he seemed interested in pursuing a relationship with her, or even seducing her. Maybe she simply wasn't his type. Maybe he liked them big and busty, like Babette. Or shallow and slinky, like Vanessa.

"I hope you're giving some thought to all the trouble

you caused tonight,'' he said as he held open the door to the apartment building.

She stopped in the doorway, turning to face him. ''Actually, I was wondering what type of woman you find attractive.''

Nick looked baffled. ''What does that have to do with the case?''

''Nothing. I was just curious.''

His eyes narrowed. ''I think you're trying to change the subject. We're talking about the stunt you pulled tonight. The one that almost put me back behind bars, thanks to Babette.''

''Did you find Babette attractive?''

''It's hard to fantasize about a woman when she's got you upside down in a bone-crunching headlock. I'll probably have nightmares about her.''

''What about Vanessa?''

''Vanessa won't give me nightmares,'' he said, leaning against the open door.

She swallowed. ''She is pretty.''

''Stunning.''

''And rich and sexy and skinny,'' Lucy muttered.

''And boring as hell.''

She blinked. ''What? You mean you didn't fall under the spell of the Wicked Witch of Westview?''

Nick shook his head as he followed her inside the building. ''She might not be guilty of arson but she could certainly bore a man to death. I could barely stay awake through the meal.'' He scowled down at her when they reached her apartment door. ''But then I realized you were off masquerading as a hooker, and perked right up again.''

''Vanessa *bored* you?'' she asked, stopping in front of her door and inserting the key into the dead bolt.

"Right up until the time she dropped the biggest clue of this case into my lap, figuratively speaking."

Lucy spun around. "A clue? Really?"

"Possibly," he amended. "But I don't want you to get your hopes up."

That was like telling her not to breathe. She threw her arms around his neck. "Oh, Nick. A clue. A real clue. A chance to save Melvin."

His arms went around her. Lucy was suddenly very aware of his earthy scent, the long, hard length of his body and the nearness of his mouth to her own. Her breath quickened. She wanted him to kiss her, to lose control. To make her forget all about her policy against ex-cons.

They backed away from each other at the same time.

Lucy's heart skipped a beat as she struggled for something to say.

"I have to go," Nick announced, his eyes half-lidded and unreadable.

"Wait a minute." She reached out to grab his forearm before he could escape. His muscles tensed under her fingertips. "What about the clue? Tell me everything."

"I don't think that's a good idea."

She dropped her hand, staring up at him in disbelief. "You're not going to tell me?"

"No."

"That's ridiculous. I have to know."

"Why? So you can hatch some new harebrained scheme?" He folded his arms across his chest. "Forget it."

She resisted the urge to stamp her foot. "But I've got a right to know. I'm paying you for information."

"You're paying me to find evidence to clear your brother of arson charges. That's what I'm doing. And the last thing I need is a lunatic librarian interfering with the case."

"Don't you think 'lunatic' is a little extreme?"

"I was being nice. You're actually the most dangerous woman I've ever met. I'm lucky to still be alive."

"You're exaggerating. And you're shutting me out of the case because of a few little mishaps."

"Mishaps? Lucy, I almost got arrested tonight—for the second time in less than two weeks. You've tried to blind me with hair spray. And don't forget about the peanut butter."

She rolled her eyes. "Well, if you're going to bring up every little incident, I could lodge a few complaints myself."

"Such as?"

"Such as...kissing me the night of the stakeout." She tipped up her chin. "I'd hardly call that professional behavior."

"As I remember it, you kissed me."

"But you kissed me back."

He rifled a hand through his short dark hair. "I've been in prison for the last fifteen months. What did you expect?"

Her cheeks grew warm. "Flattery will get you nowhere."

He opened his mouth, but she held up her hand to ward off his apology. At least she hoped it was an apology. "Let's just forget about that kiss."

"Believe me, I've tried," he muttered. "Just like I've tried to figure out how I ever got into this mess. Because when we were in the library, you looked harmless. Did you hypnotize me? Use mind control? Voodoo?"

"Quit trying to change the subject. I want to know about the new lead in the case. At least give me a hint."

"No."

"Does it involve Vanessa?" she asked, then waved her hand in the air. "What am I saying? Of course it does. She was at dinner with you tonight. She must have made some kind of slip-up. Did she say something incriminating? Reveal a motive? Use the wrong fork?"

"I'm not going to stand out in the hallway playing Twenty Questions."

"Then let's go inside," she said, placing her hand on the doorknob.

"That's not a good idea."

"I'll make coffee. We can talk about the case and plan our strategy."

"I don't drink coffee."

"Then I'll give you tea, beer, milk of magnesia—anything you want."

"How about the silent treatment?"

"You're impossible!" she exclaimed, wanting to shake him. Didn't he realize how important this was to her? How much she was willing to sacrifice for her brother? "Not to mention irritating, stubborn and evasive. Didn't they teach you any communication skills in prison?"

"I guess we were all too busy with those ballroom dance lessons."

"Well, you've got tap dancing down pat," Lucy said in a fit of exasperation. "You've avoided answering all of my questions. You won't tell me about the new clue. And I think you're trying your hardest to start an argument."

He just stood there watching her, his jaw clamped tightly shut.

"You are, aren't you?" she accused. "In fact, you've been like this ever since we met. It's like you purposely try to pick fights with me."

"You're right," he admitted, taking a step closer to her. "I do."

Suddenly Lucy became very aware of all six feet two inches of solid, potent male. She swallowed. "Why?"

"Because it keeps me from doing something stupid."

She stared up at him, confused. "Like what?"

"Like this." He lowered his head and captured her mouth with his own.

Her breath caught in her throat at the unexpected onslaught of his lips. His mouth melded against hers with raw desire and molten heat. Desire flared inside her as his arms wrapped around her waist, pulling her tightly against him.

Lucy leaned into him, her hands pressed against his chest. Her fingers flexed against hard, unyielding muscle until he moaned low into her mouth, deepening the kiss. She slid her hands up to his shoulders, wrapping them around his neck to pull him even closer. Then she held on tight as he kissed her again. She kissed him back, shutting out everything but the fierce intensity of their embrace.

When he finally ended the kiss, she could barely breathe, much less think clearly. So he did find her attractive. The very idea made her light-headed. Or maybe it was lack of oxygen. Nick was certainly taking up his fair share, breathing hard and fast, his mouth only scant inches from her own.

"Now do you understand?" he rasped, his hands gripping her shoulders. "I want you, Lucy. I want you all the time. Right now I'd like nothing better than to take you into that apartment and lock the door. To shut out the rest of the world. To keep you there, in my arms, for a week...a month...a year. I want to make love to you until we both pass out from exhaustion. And then I want to love you all over again."

His communication skills were definitely improving.

"Why..." she began, the word sticking in her parched throat. She licked her lips, unnerved by the way his gaze followed her tongue. "Why didn't you say something before?"

"Because it's impossible. You have a policy against

guys like me. And even if you didn't, I can't afford to take that kind of risk.'' He stepped away from her. ''You're trouble, Lucy Moore. You've been trouble since the first day we met.''

The loss of his body heat didn't explain the sudden chill deep inside her. He meant it. Stubborn determination steeled his gray eyes. How could he kiss her like that one moment, then want nothing to do with her the next? Was it possible that he hadn't experienced the same emotional upheaval during that kiss? Was it possible that she was falling in love with Nick Chamberlin?

Lucy sucked in her breath. ''I don't know what you mean. I've just been trying to help with the case.''

''That's the problem. From now on, I'm working solo.''

She blinked back her shock at his unexpected announcement. ''You can't be serious.''

''No more contact between us. Except by telephone. It's the only way I'll agree to keep working for you.''

She couldn't believe it. He was actually afraid of her. What next? A clove of garlic around his neck to keep her at bay? ''This is ridiculous. I'll admit I'm attracted to you, too.'' A serious understatement, considering her knees were so weak, she needed to lean against the wall to remain upright. ''If we both exercise some self-control, I'm sure we can resist temptation.''

''I can't,'' he said baldly. ''Not anymore.''

''Just until after the case,'' she promised.

A muscle flickered in his jaw. ''Nothing is going to change once the case is over. I don't want any complications in my life, and you can't risk your dreams by becoming involved with an ex-con—a dirty cop who will never be accepted in this city.''

''So you're doing this for me?'' she asked, helpless and frustrated as she saw her newest, most precious dream slipping away. The dream conceived in Nick's arms. Tears stung her eyes. "For a dirty cop, you're annoyingly noble. Besides, I'm old enough to make my own decisions."

"The decision's already made. I won't let you sacrifice your life, too."

"What does that mean?"

"Nothing. End of discussion." He reached around her to open the door. As it swung open, he turned her around and gave her a gentle shove.

She took one look inside her apartment and screamed.

7

"WOW," NICK SAID, stepping over the threshold. "This place really is a mess. Have you ever thought about hiring a cleaning service?"

"I didn't do this," she exclaimed, looking around her living room in disbelief. "I may not be Martha Stewart, but I'm not a total slob. Someone must have broken in."

She wrapped her arms around herself, attempting to ward off the cold emptiness growing inside of her. Her apartment was in total disarray. Clothes from the laundry basket she'd left by the door were strewn all over the floor. All the books from her bookshelf lay open in haphazard piles. Every drawer of the antique buffet stood open and empty, the contents of each dumped onto the carpet below.

"Don't touch anything," Nick warned just as she reached down to pick up a shattered photograph of Melvin on his motorcycle. "The police will want to check for fingerprints."

"Police." She mouthed the word under her breath, still not ready to believe this could really be happening to her.

Nick pushed her gently onto an easy chair. "You sit here while I check out the rest of the apartment."

His words had barely registered before he was back by her side. "The kitchen, bathroom and your bedroom all look like this one. The intruder was certainly thorough."

"But not very neat."

"Can you tell if anything is missing?"

She looked around the disheveled room again as the reality slowly began to sink in. "Actually, it looks like he added stuff. I can't believe all this mess belongs to me."

Then her eyes widened in horror. "Someone was inside my apartment. Do you know what that means?"

Nick nodded. "You probably feel violated."

"What I feel is embarrassed! Some total stranger saw my apartment." She closed her eyes. "All those dirty dishes on the counter. I didn't even have time to wipe off the kitchen table after breakfast this morning. And the bathroom..." She groaned and leaned her head back against the chair. "I was going to mop the floor tomorrow. Really."

"Don't be ridiculous," he snapped. "Who cares what the scum who did this thinks?"

She stood up. "I've got to clean up before the police get here."

"I told you not to touch anything."

"Just a little dusting," she said, eyeing the thick layer on top of the buffet. "Maybe give the bathtub a quick wipe."

"Lucy," he said, pulling her back down into the chair. "You can scour the place from top to bottom *after* the police check everything out. I called them from the bedroom. They should be here any minute."

"Great. First they think I'm a lousy hooker, and now they'll think I'm a lousy housekeeper." A lump lodged in her throat as she swallowed a sob.

Nick kneeled down next to her chair, gently brushing her hair off her cheek. "Everything will be all right. We'll catch the jerk who did this to you. I promise."

If only he'd hold her in his arms...make her feel safe...make her feel comforted. Make her feel like he was paying attention. "Nick?" she said, as he stared at something over her shoulder.

He stood. ''Your answering machine is blinking.'' He walked over to the telephone stand. Picking up a pencil, he pushed the play button with the tip of the eraser.

She was experiencing one of the most traumatic moments of her life, and he was worried about retrieving phone messages. ''Were you expecting a call?''

''No. But the burglar might have called earlier to make certain the apartment was empty. It's a typical M.O.''

The first message was an insurance salesman who, ironically, offered a special one-month rate against theft and burglary. The second was from Letitia Beaumont, wondering if Lucy could serve tea at the meeting of the Heritage Library Foundation.

The third caller didn't identify himself. ''Hello, Lucy,'' he said, the voice sounding muffled and far away. ''Will you pick up if you're there? Lucy? I have an important message for you. Pick up, Lucy.''

''Do you know who that was?'' Nick asked, as the answering machine beeped twice to indicate the end of the messages.

She shook her head. ''I don't think so. He doesn't sound the same.''

Nick slowly turned around to face her. ''The same as what?''

''As the other guy.'' She wrinkled her nose. ''This one sounds rougher, meaner. Floyd's voice is higher, and he has kind of an asthmatic wheeze when he talks.''

''Who is Floyd?''

''My stalker,'' she said, then shrugged her shoulders. ''Well, that's not really his name. I just call him that.''

Nick sat down on the sofa next to her chair. ''Slow down a minute. Someone is *stalking* you?''

She shrugged again. ''Well, maybe not technically stalking me. He leaves bizarre messages on my answering machine. Once in a while it seems like a light blue Ford Escort is tailing me. But there have to be hundreds of those around, right?''

''Anything else?''

''I've found footprints outside my window. But that could be the gardener or the meter man.''

''It's October, Lucy. All the plants and flowers are dead. And I saw the gas meter on the way in. It's next to the laundry room.''

''Well, there has to be a reasonable explanation for the footprints. I can't believe someone would actually spy on me.''

''How long have you been getting the phone calls?''

She thought a moment. ''Just for the past few weeks.''

''And you call this guy Floyd?'' Nick asked in a strangled voice.

''It made it all seem less scary. I didn't want to overreact to a few crank phone calls. Besides, why would anyone be stalking me?''

''Why would anyone break into your apartment?'' he asked, pacing back and forth across the living room. ''Or frame your brother? I can't believe you didn't tell me about this sooner.''

''Oh, Nick,'' she exclaimed, smiling amidst the chaos. ''This is wonderful. You finally believe someone framed Melvin.''

He stopped pacing. ''I think it's a possibility. But I don't want to talk about your brother at the moment. I want to know about Floyd—every little detail.''

''GUESS THAT ABOUT WRAPS it up,'' Lieutenant Delaney said as the evidence crew left the apartment with all their samples in tiny plastic bags. ''Are you certain nothing is missing, Miss Moore?''

"I don't know," Lucy said, hugging Sherlock to her chest. She'd finally found him underneath her bed, guarding the dust bunnies. "He didn't take my mother's pearl ring or the gold bracelet Melvin gave me for my college graduation."

"Her television set and all the appliances are still here, too," Nick added. "Seems like the perp was on a search-and-destroy mission."

"Searching for what?" she asked.

Lieutenant Delaney seated himself on the vinyl ottoman, flipping open his notebook. "That's what we need to figure out. Now Nick told me you've been receiving some unusual phone calls."

"He told you about Floyd?"

Nick rubbed his temple. Leave it to Lucy to give her stalker a name. Next, she'd be leaving him milk and cookies on the doorstep.

Lieutenant Delaney jotted the name down in his notebook. "Do you know Floyd's last name?"

"I don't even know his first name. I just call him Floyd."

Delaney looked at Nick.

"Don't ask," Nick said. "The important thing is Lucy doesn't think Floyd left the latest message on the answering machine."

Delaney nodded. "I listened to it several times. Sounds like his voice is disguised."

"Which means it could still be Floyd," Nick said.

"Or someone else she knows," Delaney added.

Lucy's mouth fell open. "You think I might know the person who did all this?" she asked, indicating the disaster area that used to be her living room.

Nick sat forward in his chair, his elbows on his knees. "Check out a guy named Walter 'Weasel' Malone," he told Delaney. "See if he can explain his whereabouts for the past eight hours."

"Weasel would never do this to me," Lucy said. "Besides, he's allergic to cat hair. He wouldn't last five minutes in here with Sherlock. It's probably just some random burglary that could have happened to anyone."

Nick turned to her. "How many burglars do you know leave the house empty-handed?"

"Number one, I don't know any burglars...anymore. And number two, my stuff isn't that nice. Maybe Jamie thought it wasn't worth the effort."

"Jamie?" Nick and Delaney said at the same time.

"I think that's what we should call him to avoid confusion," Lucy said. "Or her. After all, this is the nineties. I'm sure there are as many women in the burglary business now as there are men."

"Perhaps you should see a crisis counselor," Delaney suggested gently. "I'm sure this has been an upsetting experience for you."

Lucy blinked at him. "There's nothing wrong with me. I'm perfectly fine."

Delaney looked skeptically at Nick.

Nick gave a brief nod. "Don't worry about Lucy. She's always like this."

The lieutenant cleared his throat. "Fine. Then let's proceed. Did you leave any doors or windows unlocked today?"

"I always leave the north bedroom window open about four inches for Sherlock."

"Now wait a minute," Delaney said. "You've got a stalker named Floyd, a burglar named Jamie and now Sherlock. Who is he and what's his crime?"

"Sherlock's my cat," she explained. "And he's not guilty of anything except drooling over my neighbor's pet parakeet. He likes to lie on the windowsill and enjoy the breeze. Maybe Jamie got in that way."

Delaney jotted the information in his notepad. "Does anyone else have a key to your apartment?"

Lucy nibbled her lip. "Melvin did have one, but he gave it back to me after his arrest. Oh, and I used to have a roommate."

"Male or female."

Lucy could feel Nick tense beside her. "Female," she said. "Barbara moved to England last year."

"I think you should make a list of all your friends and acquaintances," Nick suggested. "And anyone who might hold a grudge against you."

"Jamie probably doesn't even know me," Lucy said, not wanting to believe any of her friends could do this to her. "What if he lost his job and has three small, hungry children and a pregnant wife? Desperation drove him to break into my apartment, but then he came to his senses and—"

"Lucy," Nick interjected, his voice hard-edged and impatient, "this isn't some fairy tale. This is real life. Someone broke into your apartment. A criminal. A thief. A murderer, for all we know. When I think you could have been alone here with him..."

"Miss Moore's wild imagination seems to be contagious," Delaney said. "I deal in facts. Someone broke into your apartment, went through everything with a fine-tooth comb but took nothing. Which means he didn't find what he was looking for."

"But what was he looking for?" Lucy asked. "I don't have anything valuable."

Nick turned to her. "The evidence."

Her mouth fell open. "From Goldie's gossip column?"

"Is this the column that claimed you found new evidence in the case against Melvin Moore?"

"You saw it, too?" Nick asked the detective.

Delaney snorted. "It was big news down at the station. You know cops don't like to be accused of shoddy investigating—especially Cole Rafferty."

"I wanted to flush out the real arsonist," Lucy explained. "Goldie offered to help me."

"And that's when you told her about this new evidence?" Delaney asked. "The proof that can set your brother free?"

"It does exist," Lucy insisted. "I just haven't found it yet. But I was hoping the real arsonist would panic and do something stupid—reveal himself."

"Looks like he panicked all right," Nick said.

Delaney tapped his pen against the notepad. "So let me get this straight. You made it all up? There is no new evidence in the case?"

"That's why the burglar left empty-handed," Nick concluded. "But that doesn't mean he won't be back." He turned to Delaney. "I think Lucy should be under police protection."

Delaney shook his head. "We just don't have that kind of manpower, Chamberlin. Unless you want me to put her in the lockup—for her own protection."

Lucy shot to her feet. She knew Nick wanted to be rid of her, but locking her away seemed a little extreme. "One Moore in your jail is already one too many. You can't put me there against my will."

"She's right about that," Delaney agreed, "although I think it may be for the best."

Lucy shook her head. "No way."

Nick stood up and folded his arms across his chest, stubbornness practically oozing from every pore. "Then I've got an even better idea."

"THIS IS NICKY'S ROOM," Sadie said, leading Lucy into a large attic bedroom with a double bed and a dresser tucked in one corner. A round stained-glass window spilled a rainbow of colors on the polished hardwood floor. "You can unpack while I make us a nice pot of chicken gumbo for dinner."

"I don't know how to thank you," Lucy said, setting down her suitcase, her legs still shaky from the shock of seeing her home torn apart. "I still think Nick's overreacting, but he wouldn't take no for an answer. He insisted I stay with you while he camps out at my apartment."

"He does have a stubborn streak."

"Tell me about it." Lucy sat down on the bed, then plopped backward, sinking into the downy comforter. "He never listens to a word I say. He's bossy and opinionated and bullheaded."

"All the things I love about him," Sadie chimed. "But he has his faults, too."

"What if the burglar does come back to my apartment?" Lucy asked, voicing the fear that had been niggling at her for the last hour. "Nick could be in danger."

"Don't worry. My grandson knows how to take care of himself." Sadie stepped back and eyed Lucy from head to toe. "I think it will just about fit."

"What?" she asked, distracted by the scent of Nick on the bedcovers. It made her stomach flip-flop to think of him sleeping here, cozy and rumpled and practically naked. Unless he slept in pajamas. But for some reason, pajamas and Nick Chamberlin just didn't seem to go together.

"My wedding dress. We might have to take up the hem a bit, but otherwise I think it will be perfect."

Lucy sat up. "Your wedding dress?"

"It's a long satin gown. Very simple. Nothing elaborate or fussy." Sadie tapped her chin with one finger. "And I think a circlet of delicate silk flowers for your hair. Or would you prefer a veil?''

''Sadie, I'm not planning a wedding.''

''Oh, I know that, dear. Not yet. First we have to settle this little mix-up with your brother. But once he's out of jail, there's no reason for you and Nicky to wait any longer.''

''Me and Nicky?'' Lucy squeaked. She'd imagined herself married someday. When the right man came along. But that man couldn't be Nick, with his unsavory background and dead-end future. *Could it?* Just the thought of spending the rest of her days and nights with him made her feel dizzy. Probably not a good sign.

''You two are made for each other. I've never seen Nicky as animated as he is around you. He can't take his eyes off you.''

''I think it's a form of self-defense. He still hasn't forgotten about that peanut butter incident.'' Lucy stared up at the thin, jagged crack in the plaster ceiling, wondering how many times Nick had stared up at the same crack, wondering how many dreams he'd made for himself while lying awake in this bed.

Had any of his dreams ever come true?

''You'll both laugh about it someday.'' Sadie moved over to the closet, making room on the rod for Lucy's clothes. ''Nicky has a wonderful sense of humor.''

She'd rarely even seen him smile. But the few times he had, her knees had gone weak. Nick revealed himself to her in bits and pieces, like a jigsaw puzzle that promises a great picture, but drives you crazy as you try to put it together.

Now he didn't even want to see her again, much less marry her. He'd made that perfectly clear after kissing her senseless outside her front door.

"Nicky doesn't want you to tell anyone you're staying here," Sadie reminded her. "He'll forward your mail and relay any important phone calls. And you're not to go anywhere except work without his permission."

"This is ridiculous," Lucy cried, frustrated with Nick and the way her life was spinning out of control. She didn't know what she wanted anymore. "I'm twenty-eight years old. I'm a college graduate. I'm an honorary member of the Book-of-the-Month Club. He can't tell me what to do!"

"Take it from me, Lucy," Sadie said, patting her shoulder sympathetically. "Never argue with a Chamberlin man. It's a waste of breath."

"YOU'RE WASTING your breath, Chamberlin," Cole Rafferty said the next morning. He sat with his feet propped on the desk while he munched on a doughnut. "A matchbook isn't exactly a written confession. You never would have released a suspect on such flimsy evidence. Bring me something more solid and we can reopen the investigation."

"We've got a tip," Nick announced. "There may be an eyewitness. A woman who saw the man that started that fire."

Cole's eyes widened. "Now this is what I mean by solid. Give me something I can go on. Have you got a name?"

Nick shook his head. "Not yet. But I've got this." He flipped the matchbook Vanessa had given him onto the desk. "Harold and Letitia Beaumont, Happy Fortieth Wedding Anniversary. April nineteenth. The same night as the fire. Now tell me how an identical matchbook ended up in the Hanover Building?"

Cole stared at the matchbook on his desk, then shrugged. "It could have belonged to Mad Dog himself. You know the guys in the lab couldn't find any prints."

"Mad Dog wasn't at the party."

Cole pulled his feet off the desk, sitting straight up in his chair. "He wasn't *invited.* But we both know someone with Mad Dog's background isn't adverse to crashing a party."

"Then let's interview the guests to see if anyone spotted him there. Did you get the list?"

Cole shook his head as he licked powdered sugar off his fingertips. "Nope. The Beaumonts disposed of the invitation list shortly after the party. According to Mrs. Beaumont, over two hundred people were invited." Cole sighed. "My invitation must have gotten lost in the mail."

"The Beaumonts were probably afraid you'd charm the designer stockings off their daughter. Of course, they don't know you like I do."

"Hey," Cole said, holding up both hands, "I'd know better than to abscond with Mad Dog Moore's woman. I value my life."

"Maybe that's it," Nick ventured. "One of those smooth, preppy boys fell for Vanessa but couldn't compete with Mad Dog, so he decided to get him out of the way."

"I think you've been spending too much time with that lovely librarian. That scenario sounds straight out of a mystery novel."

Nick had to agree. He was getting desperate for an explanation, any explanation other than the one Lucy didn't want to hear—that her brother was guilty of arson. If only they had something more concrete to go on. So far, all their investigation had turned up was a couple matchbooks and a possible unknown eyewitness with a flower name. Hardly enough to justify reopening the investigation.

He rubbed his jaw, frustrated with his lack of progress in the case. "Can you come up with a better scenario?"

Cole grinned. "Maybe Floyd and Jamie teamed up to do it."

Nick folded his arms across his chest. "Very funny. I take it Delaney can't keep his big mouth shut?"

Cole shook his head. "That Lucy is priceless. Not to mention creative, sweet and incredibly sexy in a red wig. Are you *sure* she doesn't have a sister?"

"Believe me," Nick said, pocketing the matchbook, "Lucy is one of a kind."

"GOOD AFTERNOON, LADIES," Lucy said, hurrying into the Monday-afternoon meeting of the Merry Widows Book Club. "I'm so sorry I'm late. We've got several new patrons, so we're busier than usual around here today."

"How nice," Veda said. "Mr. Bonn must be pleased."

Lucy just smiled as she took her seat. Lester wasn't pleased. In fact, he was mortified. Most of the new patrons were people Lucy recruited the night she went undercover as a prostitute. They'd brought in their children for the reading hour and signed up for library cards and had the library director scurrying to the telephone to call his mother. He didn't like change, believing the library to be an almost sacred institution.

He reminded her of the starchy librarian she'd been terrified of as a small child. The one who had always made Lucy and the other kids from Bale Street wash their hands before they touched any of the books.

Lester had looked like he wanted to scour the library from floor to ceiling with disinfectant. Fortunately for him, the library closed at six o'clock on Monday evenings so they could find room in the tight city budget to be open on Sunday afternoons. He only had to handle three more hours of these unconventional library patrons. Though Lucy sincerely hoped they returned to take advantage of all the Heritage Library had to offer.

An empty chair caught her attention. "Where's Sadie?"

"That's what we were wondering," Edith said. "We can't start the meeting without her. She has to read the minutes."

Lucy blinked. "Minutes? But we're a book club. We don't have minutes."

"We do now, dear," Veda said, pulling out her knitting needles. "We voted Sadie in as secretary after our last meeting."

"Oh," Lucy said, still confused. "Why?"

"Some of us suffer from short-term memory loss," Goldie explained in a whisper.

Lenora Eberly bristled. "I may be forgetful, but I'm not deaf. Besides, I think it's a good idea to keep a record of our meetings."

"Especially since they've gotten so exciting lately," Edith piped up.

Goldie turned to Lucy. "You can bring us up-to-date while we wait for Sadie. Tell us everything." The small circle of women fluttered with anticipation.

Lucy didn't know where to begin. "Well...we still haven't found the real arsonist, but he did break into my apartment because of that item you planted in your column."

Goldie clapped her hands. "That's wonderful!"

Lucy nodded. "Actually, it is. Because now Nick really believes Mad Dog is innocent. Of course, he also thinks I might be in danger, so he forced me to move out of my own home. And he won't tell me about the new lead in the case."

"Isn't that romantic?" Veda cried. "He's trying to protect you."

Or avoid her. She hadn't even seen him since the night of their arrest two whole days ago. Ignoring her might work for Nick, but it only made Lucy very aware of how much she missed him. It probably didn't help matters that she'd been sleeping in his bed, wrapping her arms around his pillow every night just to breathe in his scent. Pathetic, but true.

"The problem is that I want to help solve this case," Lucy said. "But Nick just won't listen to reason."

"He is a man, dear," Lenora reminded her.

Edith nodded. "Just give him some time. He'll come around to your way of thinking."

"They always do," Veda added. "Love makes people act pretty crazy sometimes."

"But we're not in love," Lucy protested, feeling a telltale blush creep into her cheeks.

They all smiled and Goldie winked at her. She was outnumbered. A dozen reasons why she couldn't love Nick Chamberlin battled on the tip of her tongue: his prison record, his sullied reputation, his uncertain future. But they didn't seem to matter much anymore. Not when she thought about the Nick she'd come to know. How he took care of his grandmother, sang show tunes...kissed with a consuming intensity that made her cheeks burn just to think about it.

She fanned a sheet of paper in front of her face, ready to introduce a safer topic, like fictional serial killers, when she saw Lester in the doorway, waving frantically at her.

Excusing herself, she walked over to him. "What is it, Lester?"

"Another one of *those women* has arrived," he hissed, motioning behind him. A petite young woman with straight, blond hair that reached almost to her waist stood next to the huge globe in the corner.

"Mother said I'm not to associate with anyone wearing leather or a nose ring," he said, his thin lips pinched with disapproval. "Since you're responsible for bringing this rabble to the library, you can deal with it. I'll send Mindy up to handle your book club duties."

Lucy bit back an angry retort. "Fine. I'll be more than happy to assist her."

Lester sniffed. "Wait until Mrs. Beaumont hears about all this," he mumbled as he strode away.

Lucy sighed inwardly, used to Lester's dissatisfaction with her unorthodox ideas. Over the years, he'd submitted a series of complaints about her. The last typed report critiquing her conduct had been four single-spaced pages long.

Telling herself to forget about her problems with Lester, she turned to the waiflike woman in the baggy blue sweater and skin-tight black leather pants. The flush in the girl's cheeks told Lucy she'd overheard Lester's tantrum.

"I'm Lucy," she said with a welcoming smile. "How can I help you, Miss…?"

"Vyne," the girl said softly. "But you can call me Lily."

8

LUCY'S HEART SKIPPED a beat. "Lily?"

She nodded. "I heard you were looking for me. One of the girls gave me a bookmark with the name and address of this place. I thought the library might be a safe place to..." Her voice trailed off and her blue eyes grew wide with apprehension as voices sounded in the stairwell.

Lucy pulled her into the audiovisual room, closing the door behind them. "We can have some privacy in here," she said, flipping on the lights. Then she turned around. "You're the one, aren't you? The eyewitness."

Lily sank into a chair. "I know Melvin didn't start that fire."

"You call him Melvin?" Lucy hadn't heard anyone call him by his real name for years. When he was twelve he'd earned the moniker Mad Dog by facing down a vicious street mongrel and coming out on top. During his teen years, he spent most of his time in trouble, just trying to live up to his reputation. Only Lucy had known there was really a sweet puppy dog beneath all that bluster.

A rosy blush suffused Lily's pale cheeks. "He asked me to call him Melvin. I'd see him sometimes on the street. Not that he ever wanted to do any...business. Melvin was always very kind to me."

Lucy's heart melted. "I'm glad. My brother may act tough, but he's really just a big pushover—especially for a pretty girl."

Lily's blush deepened. "He always treated me like a lady. I couldn't believe it when they arrested him."

Lucy slid into the chair next to her. "Why didn't you come forward? Try to help Melvin? Go to the police and tell them what you saw?"

"No one would have believed me."

"I'm sure that's not true."

"I am." Lily chewed on her lower lip. "The guy wore a tuxedo that night, but I still recognized him. He didn't see me standing there in the shadows. Shortly after he left Melvin's place, I saw smoke rolling out of the windows." She twisted her fingers in her lap. "I called 911 from the phone booth on the corner to report the fire. Then I ran."

"Oh, Lily, you recognized him!" Her mind raced to absorb this new information. *A tuxedo?* Fancy dress for such dirty work. "Now we can nail the real arsonist. You can identify him...."

Lily shot to her feet. "No. I can't."

"I'll go down to the police station with you," Lucy promised. "You can tell them who you saw. Then all you'll probably have to do is pick him out of a lineup."

Lily emphatically shook her head and started backing toward the door. "I've probably said too much already. If he finds out..."

Lucy rose. "But Lily, you may be the only one who can help Melvin."

"I'm sorry," Lily cried. "I can't. I just...can't." Then she turned and bolted out the door.

Lucy raced after her, knowing she might never see her again if Lily didn't want to be found. Her heels skidded on the polished tile floor as she rounded the corner. She slammed straight into a hard, broad chest that emitted a resounding "Ooomph!"

"Sorry," she gasped, her gaze still on Lily's retreating

back. She tried to step away, but two strong arms held her firmly in place. She looked up to find Nick gazing down at her with molten gray eyes.

"We've got to stop meeting like this," he said.

She pointed toward the swinging library door. "That was her. That was the eyewitness!"

"Marigold?"

"Her name is Lily," she said, very aware of the heat of his body and the way his long fingers spanned her waist. She took a step away from him so she could think more clearly.

Nick was still staring at the door. "I can't believe it. Weasel actually gave us a legitimate tip. Do you want me to go after her?"

"No," Lucy said, really wanting him to hold her again. But she had to think of her brother first. Even if just the sight of Nick Chamberlin made her heart thump in her chest.

She took another step back from him, still not quite trusting herself. "What are you doing here?"

He held up a canvas tote bag. "Gram forgot her books. I thought she might want them for the meeting."

"I'm sure she will, but she isn't here yet."

He frowned. "That's impossible. She said she had a ride to the library. And I found the tote bag sitting out on the front stoop."

Lucy motioned toward the open door of the meeting room. "See for yourself. Everybody's here but Sadie."

Nick looked in the room, then looked at Lucy. "If she's not here, then where the hell is she?"

She shrugged. "I don't know. She never misses a book club meeting. Maybe we should ask the other members. They might have talked to her."

Lester rounded the corner. ''Excuse me, Miss Moore. You have a telephone call.''

Lucy looked up at Nick. ''I'd better take it.''

He nodded. ''Go ahead. I'll ask the ladies if any of them have talked to Gram today. If they don't know anything, I'm contacting the police.'' He rubbed one hand over his midsection. ''I have a bad feeling about this.''

So did Lucy. She hurried to the telephone, telling herself not to worry—only she knew Sadie never missed a meeting of the Merry Widows. Anxiety trickled through her as she stepped over two toddlers to reach for the phone. ''Hello?''

''Lucy, thank God. I thought I'd never find you.'' The masculine voice on the other end sounded strained, yet familiar.

''Weasel?'' she guessed.

''Yeah, it's me. I've been trying to reach you all afternoon.''

''Weasel, turn your television down,'' she said. ''I can hardly hear you.''

''I said I've been looking for you everywhere,'' he yelled. ''That twit who answers the phone kept saying you can't receive personal calls. I finally told him it was an emergency.''

Lucy's heart froze in her chest. ''An emergency? Oh my God! Is it Melvin?'' Her two weeks weren't up yet. Had he gotten impatient? Made his prison break early? She sucked in her breath. ''Has something happened to him?''

''No, no, nothing like that.'' He paused a moment, and she could hear strains of music playing in the background. ''But you've got to get over here.''

''Where are you?''

''My place. The apartment on Bale Street. Number 503.''

She twisted the phone cord in her fingers. ''This really isn't a good time....''

''Please come, Luce,'' he said as the music blared louder. ''Please. I...don't know what else to do.''

The hairs prickled on the back of her neck. But it wasn't Weasel's frantic, harassed tone that unnerved her. It was the music she heard on the other end of the line, the music she finally recognized. The theme song to *Oklahoma.*

''I'll be there in ten minutes.''

ONE HOUR and one flat tire later, Lucy arrived on Bale Street. It looked the same as it had when she was ten years old. There was still litter in the streets, gang members on the corners, and a sign in Rigetto's Bakery window offering free weight-loss classes.

Apartment buildings lined the rest of the block—tall, stark brick structures with broken windows and graffiti sprayed on the front stoops. Her old house had been torn down long ago, replaced by a Jiffy Lube. Even with all the changes in her life, part of her would always think of this street as home. Growing up here had made her both strong and stubborn. More importantly, it had taught her to dream.

Only now, her dreams went beyond a successful career and a house in a nice neighborhood. She wanted family around her. Not only Melvin, free and happy, but a family of her own—a husband and children, a house that was really a home and a kind of love she'd never dared dream of before. The kind of love that survived whether you lived on Bale Street or the Eagle Estates. The kind of love she had for Nick.

Reconciled with her past and optimistic about her future, she strode into Weasel's apartment building, smiling at the ragtag little girl of about nine standing just inside the front door.

''Hey, lady,'' the girl said, her chin jutting out, her wispy blond braids falling over her shoulders. "Wanna buy a genuine gold bracelet? Only twenty bucks."

Lucy looked at the tin bracelet in the girl's grubby hand. She'd bet a lot more than twenty bucks that the *genuine gold* bracelet would turn her wrist green in less than a day. She knew a con when she saw one. And she also knew no one on Bale Street respected a sucker.

"Twenty bucks for that Cracker Jack toy?" Lucy replied skeptically. "I won't pay a dime over ten."

"Deal," the girl said instantly, trying to hide a toothy grin.

"You didn't let me finish," Lucy said, trying to hide a grin of her own. "I'll pay you five dollars now and the another five when you show up at the Heritage Library and check out a certain book that I know a smart girl like you will just love. I'm a librarian there and read the same book when I was about your age."

The little girl shrewdly eyed Lucy's tailored silk suit. "Make it ten bucks when I check out that book, and you've got a deal."

"Deal," Lucy said, exchanging the cheap bracelet for a crisp five-dollar bill and knowing the little girl would be getting something so much more out of the bargain. This is what Lucy wanted to do with her life: help people find their dreams.

As she rode the elevator up five floors, she added to the graffiti on the walls. With a red flair pen she wrote: For A Good Time, Call This Number. Then she printed the Heritage library's telephone number below.

She just hoped Lester didn't find out about her newest promotional idea.

When she reached the fifth floor, Lucy walked down the long, narrow hallway, looking for her destination. To her surprise, the door to apartment 503 stood wide open. Most residents of Bale Street knew not only to lock their door, but to invest in a deadbolt, chain lock, motion alarm, and if they were smart, a hungry pit bull.

Nobody left their door wide open.

Lucy stepped gingerly over the threshold, impressed by the spotless appearance of the living room and tiny kitchen nook. The roar of a vacuum cleaner sounded from a back bedroom. "Weasel?" she called.

When no one answered, she seated herself on the threadbare sofa to wait until he finished. She'd never known him to be meticulously neat, but perhaps he had changed over the years...or developed an obsessive-compulsive disorder.

She picked up a magazine off the polished coffee table, flipping through the pages of *The Mercenary Gazette.* It was filled with articles on all the latest assault weapons as well as letters from mercenary enthusiasts. Correct grammar and spelling obviously weren't high on their list of requirements.

"Lucy."

She looked up to see Weasel standing at the front door, a bag of groceries in each arm.

"Thank God you're here," he said, setting the bags on the coffee table. "What took you so long?"

"I had a flat tire," she explained. "The door was open so I just walked in. I thought you were vacuuming." They both turned toward the noise emanating from the back room.

He groaned. "So she's still here."

"Who? Your mother?"

He shook his head. "Worse."

"Who could possibly be worse than your mother?" Lucy asked, remembering the acerbic Mrs. Malone.

Weasel sat down on the sofa, burying his head in his

hands. "I don't know how I ever got into this mess. A few easy bucks isn't worth what I've been through."

Lucy sat down next to him, almost afraid to voice her worst fears. "It's Sadie Chamberlin, isn't it? You've got her here."

He nodded, his face still hidden.

"You kidnapped her," she breathed. "*You really kidnapped her.* I can't believe it. Weasel, how could you ever do such a thing?"

Raising his head, he took a deep breath. "I didn't kidnap her. I'm just...detaining her for a while. She was delivered this morning. My instructions were to keep her here until further notice."

"Instructions? From whom?"

He shrugged. "I don't know his name. Some guy who calls me whenever he wants a job done."

She shot to her feet. "Like kidnapping? I thought you went straight, Weasel."

"I did. *I am.* I usually turn him down when he calls. I've certainly never done anything like this before." He wrung his hands together. "But this job came up and the money was too good to turn down. I want to get out of this neighborhood, Lucy, just like you did. And I might have a chance if my book is a hit. But I need some fast cash to cover printing and promotional expenses."

She blinked back her surprise. "Book? What book?"

A blush stained the skin under his whiskers. "I write...poems. My publisher says they're good, but he's just got a small press. If I want good distribution, I have to kick in some bucks."

"Oh, Weasel," she said, sinking back down onto the sofa. "There are other ways to get money. Grants, loans, a second job. I've heard they have an opening at Farley's Fish Hut."

"For minimum wage? That would take forever. I'm already thirty years old. Sometimes I think I'll never get out of this neighborhood." He rubbed his temple with his fingertips. "This was my ticket out, Luce."

Her pity for him turned to anger when she remembered exactly what he'd done. "By manhandling a defenseless old woman? Poor Sadie! Not only have you kept her locked away here against her will, you're forcing her to clean your apartment."

"You don't understand...."

"Oh, I understand." She leapt to her feet. "I understand that Nick was right. You're still a two-bit hood. And I've been defending you!"

He rose with his hands up, backing away from her as she stalked toward him. "Now wait a minute...."

"If you've harmed one hair on her head..." she warned.

"I'd never do that."

"But you'd make her grandson go crazy with worry," she accused, grappling in her purse for her hair spray. "And you'd make Sadie feel alone and afraid."

Weasel tripped over a footstool, falling to the floor. "I'm the one who's afraid," he clarified, holding one arm up in self-defense. "I'm afraid she'll never leave. In the last few hours, Sadie Chamberlin has made my life a living hell."

Lucy lowered the hair spray. "What are you talking about?"

He swallowed. "She's driving me crazy. Why do you think the door is wide open? For fresh air? I've tried everything to get her out of here. I even called her a taxi."

"You expect me to believe that?"

"It's true! She took control as soon as she stepped over the threshold. She made me watch *Oklahoma.*" He ran a shaky hand over his forehead. "And now I can't get those songs out of my head!"

She took a step back. "You let her watch *Oklahoma?*"

He snorted. "*Let her?* I haven't *let* her do anything. She just does exactly what she wants to do. If you don't believe me, just ask her." He hitched his thumb toward the hallway.

Lucy looked up to see Sadie pushing the upright vacuum cleaner toward a corner closet.

"Lucy," Sadie exclaimed with a wide smile. "What a nice surprise. Walter, get up off that floor. I just vacuumed in here. And take those shoes off. I told you I want to give them a good polish."

"But they're tennis shoes," he squeaked, rising to his feet. "*Canvas* tennis shoes."

"And just think how nice and bright they'll look after I whiten them up." She set the vacuum cleaner in the closet, then shut the door. "Oh, by the way, I told your next-door neighbor, Vinnie, to keep the noise down or you'd be over to teach him a lesson. And I strongly suggested he take a bath."

He gulped. "Vinnie the Viper?"

"Is that what was tattooed on his chest? I thought it was a caterpillar. It was hard to tell with all those chains."

An oven timer chimed from the kitchen. "There are my sticky buns," Sadie said, moving toward the kitchen. Then she turned to Weasel. "I put that prune sauce in the refrigerator for you. That should help take care of that little problem we talked about earlier."

When she was out of the room, Weasel turned to Lucy. "You've got to help me. Please take her with you. I'll never do anything like this again. I've learned my lesson."

"Then prove it," Lucy replied, still upset with him. "Tell me who hired you to do his dirty work."

Weasel sank down onto the sofa. "I already told you I

don't know his name. But I think he's connected to the Protégé Project."

Lucy sat down next to him. "The Protégé Project? But that doesn't make any sense. They hire people to mow lawns and paint houses, not commit felonies."

Weasel shrugged. "All I know is that every once in a while, me or one of the other guys in the program gets a call to do a job that pays a heck of a lot more than parking cars."

What could be going on? Whatever it was, Weasel did seem genuinely remorseful. She almost couldn't blame him for succumbing to temptation. She knew that burning desire to get off Bale Street, to make a better life for yourself. But just how far would Weasel go? She leveled her gaze on him. "So did this mystery man send you to the Hanover Building the same night Nick and I were there?"

"No. Mad Dog sent me there to get the keys and title to his car. He wanted to sell it so you wouldn't have to pay his legal fees." He sighed. "And I know what you're thinking, Luce. But I didn't start that fire, either."

Lucy stood up. "I don't know what to think. And what am I going to tell Nick?"

"I don't know...I don't care at this point." Weasel wrung his hands together. "Just take that woman with you."

They both looked up as Sadie walked back into the living room, wiping her hands on a dish towel. "Sticky buns, anyone?"

"Why don't we go home now, Sadie?" Lucy suggested. "You've done enough work for one day."

"I've barely scratched the surface," Sadie replied. "Poor Walter needs a woman's touch around here. I could probably stay a month and find plenty to keep me busy."

Weasel visibly paled.

"But Nick's worried sick about you," Lucy said. "He thinks...you've been kidnapped."

Sadie frowned. "Now that's just plain silly. A taxicab arrived at the house this morning, and the driver told me I'd won a free ride. Does that sound like kidnapping?"

"No," Lucy admitted. "But it does sound a little odd."

Sadie nodded. "The cab dropped me off in front of the building and Walter met me at the front door. I thought it was all part of that community mentor program I signed up for at the library."

"And I can't thank you enough," Weasel said, pulling Sadie toward the door. "Really. This is a day I'll never forget."

Sadie patted his cheek. "You are such a sweet boy. And I think with a proper haircut, you'd be a real charmer."

Weasel reached for his ponytail. "Haircut?"

"I'll bring my scissors next time," Sadie promised.

"Next time?" he squeaked.

"And you can keep that copy of *Oklahoma* until then."

"Oh, no," he protested. "I absolutely couldn't do that."

"Of course you can. I've got two more copies at home. Work on those dance steps, too. You almost had it this afternoon."

"Maybe you can teach me a few, Sadie," Lucy said as they walked out the door. She had a feeling she'd need them when she tried to explain all this to Nick.

"LET'S GO OVER our story one more time," Lucy said as she and Sadie hovered in the darkness outside the back door of Sadie's house.

"You really think Nicky will be upset?"

Lucy rolled her eyes. "Upset? I think he'll be homicidal, especially when he finds out Weasel is the reason you've been missing for the last several hours. I just hope he hasn't called the police yet."

"Oh, dear," Sadie murmured. "And Walter is such a sweet boy. I think he just needs a little attention."

"Well, he'll get plenty of attention if Nick has him arrested for kidnapping," Lucy replied. She knew Weasel had screwed up, but didn't he deserve a second chance? Just like Melvin? *Just like Nick?*

"Kidnapping?" Sadie echoed. "Now that's just plain silly. Perhaps the circumstances of my meeting Walter were a little unusual, but I like to think it was fate. It felt nice to be needed. And I was never held there against my will. Walter made it perfectly clear to me that I was free to leave. In fact, he mentioned it several times."

"Nick might not see it that way. In fact, I can almost guarantee it."

"Then we simply won't tell him."

"So we're agreed? No matter what happens, we won't mention Weasel's name?"

"Agreed." Sadie reached out to pat Lucy's cheek. "Don't look so worried, dear. I can be very creative. Now let's go in and put Nicky out of his misery."

Nick did look miserable when Lucy walked into the living room with Sadie close behind her. He sat on the sofa, his face buried in his hands. Obviously lost in his thoughts, he didn't even look up as they entered the room.

"Hi, honey, we're home," Lucy announced, hoping to lighten the tense atmosphere blanketing the room.

He slowly lifted his head, his gray eyes bleak and haggard. He looked from Lucy to his grandmother, and back again. "Where the hell have you two been?"

"Now, Nicky," Sadie said, hanging her purse on the coatrack, "you know how I feel about cursing. We're back now, that's all that matters." She took off her blue cardigan sweater and hung it next to her purse. "You must be hungry. Shall I warm up that leftover Stroganoff?"

"That's sounds wonderful," Lucy exclaimed. "Beef Stroganoff is one of my favorites."

He scowled at Lucy. "Stroganoff? *Stroganoff?* Gram disappears without a trace. Then you disappear from the library, leaving me some vague note about running an errand. I don't hear a word from either of you for hours, and now all you two can talk about is Stroganoff?"

"Well, if you don't want Stroganoff, I've got Swedish meatballs in the freezer," Sadie replied.

He closed his eyes. Lucy could see the muscle working in his tightly clenched jaw. "I don't want Swedish meatballs and I don't want Stroganoff. All I want is an explanation."

"We can do that." Sadie looked over at Lucy. "Right?"

"Right," Lucy agreed, scrambling for a plausible explanation that would keep Weasel from writing his poetry behind bars. "Sadie was...auditioning roles for a possible community theater production of *Oklahoma.*"

"I need to find someone to play Judd," Sadie explained, taking it from there. "Nicky, you'll play the hero Curly. You already know all the songs and are certainly handsome enough for the part. And Lucy, you'll be perfect in the role of Laurie."

"And you can play Aunt Eller," Lucy suggested.

Sadie shook her head. "No, dear. I'll be too busy directing. Veda will make a good Aunt Eller and Edith can do the costuming. She's an excellent seamstress."

"Hold it." Nick stood up. He didn't look convinced by their story. Harassed, impatient and incredibly sexy, but not convinced. "Look, you two," he said, his voice low and urgent, "no more games. I need to know everything. And I mean *right now.*"

Lucy bit her lip. She'd never been a good liar. Obviously Nick had seen right through her. And maybe he did need to know. No harm had come to Sadie today, but what if someone other than Weasel had been hired to *detain* her? Sadie might truly be in danger.

"You're not going to like it..." Lucy began.

"That's a given," he said, his voice tight.

"I really think it's better if you just let it go, Nicky," Sadie said. "Lucy and I agreed to keep this little episode between ourselves."

"Episode?" he echoed, his voice strained. "Is that what you call it? An...episode?"

"Nick, it's not as bad as you think," Lucy interjected. "I think Sadie even enjoyed herself."

"I really did..." Sadie began, before the chime of the doorbell interrupted her. She turned toward the door. "Well, it looks like we've got company."

"It's not company," Nick said grimly. "It's the police."

NICK WATCHED Lucy's face turn pale at his announcement. It confirmed his worst suspicions, making his gut clench and twist into a hard knot. A harried Lester Bonn had called the house fifteen minutes ago to announce that the police were on their way over. They'd come to the library looking for Lucy and he'd given him this address. One question had played over and over in his mind since that phone call.

What had she done now?

But before he could ask her, Sadie escorted two uniformed police officers into the room. He recognized the freckle-faced Officer Madison from their encounter outside the Hanover Building. And he'd never forget Babette.

"Good evening, folks. I'm Officer Madison," the young cop said, then motioned to his partner. "And this is..."

"Babette," Lucy said in surprise.

"I prefer Officer Gryzynski," Babette said as she pulled a notepad and pencil out of her pocket. "We'd like to ask you a few questions, Miss Moore."

"What k-kind of questions?" Lucy stammered, seating herself next to Nick on the sofa.

Office Madison exchanged glances with Babette. "We'd like to ask you about your activities earlier today."

"Look, this really isn't necessary," Lucy replied. "Sadie's here now. She's fine. We appreciate all your efforts, but I'm afraid you've been called out on a false alarm. I'm sure you've got more important things to do."

"Unless you'd like to stay for Stroganoff," Sadie offered. "I've got plenty to go around."

"No, thank you, ma'am," Officer Madison replied. "Officer Gryzynski and I are still on duty. We've got a job to do. And we won't rest until this case is closed."

Nick rolled his eyes. Great. Two rookie cops who had weaned themselves on reruns of "Dragnet." He knew the department was shorthanded, but this was ridiculous.

Babette tapped her pencil on the notepad. "Earlier today, Vanessa Beaumont's residence was broken into and burglarized."

Lucy blinked. "What does that have to do with me?"

"We'd like to know your whereabouts from 4:00 p.m. until now," Officer Madison replied.

Nick stifled a groan. *Burglary?* How was she ever going to talk herself out of that one?

"Lucy was with me," Sadie announced. "I was rehearsing the song-and-dance numbers from the musical *Oklahoma* with a very nice young man. He has a strong voice, although he had a little trouble with some of the steps."

Nick closed his eyes. Their story sounded lame even to

his ears. But maybe the inexperienced cops wouldn't notice. Or see the guilt written all over Lucy's face.

Babette's gaze narrowed on Lucy. "Are you sure you want to stick with that story, Miss Moore? We all know you've been pursuing an investigation to clear your brother's name."

"In fact, the first time I met you," Officer Madison said, "you'd just broken into the Hanover Building looking for evidence."

"I told you that was a misunderstanding."

Babette snorted. "Right. Just like your jaunt as a hooker was a misunderstanding. What other illegal activities have you indulged in to help your brother?"

"Now wait a minute," Lucy said, rising to her feet. "You've got it all wrong."

"We don't think so, Miss Moore," Babette countered, flipping through her notepad. "We think you spent the afternoon attempting to frame Miss Beaumont. We even have a quote from your superior at the Heritage Library, Lester Bonn. He overheard you refer to Vanessa Beaumont as the Wicked Witch of Westview. He also said you believed she was responsible for the fire."

"I never told him that," Lucy said, indignant. "You're accusing me of a crime just on Lester's word?"

"No," Officer Madison said, deadly serious behind all his freckles. "We've got more solid evidence. The perpetrator left something behind at Miss Beaumont's town house."

"Two things, actually," Babette said.

"The first is a tin of gunpowder, the same brand used in the Hanover Building fire. Obviously meant to implicate Miss Beaumont in the incident."

"And the second?" Nick demanded, suddenly hopeful that the evidence against Lucy was all circumstantial, that these two rookies had nothing more to go on than a theory and a quote from a wimpy library gossip.

"We found a fingernail file with a mother-of-pearl handle still stuck in the keyhole," Office Madison said. "I knew it looked familiar."

"But my fingernail file is one of a kind," Lucy protested.

Office Madison arched a sandy eyebrow as he held up a plastic evidence bag. "With the initial *L* etched in it?"

Lucy's mouth dropped open. She looked at Nick, her expression one of horrified disbelief.

Nick's heart lurched. If it was true, his librarian had gotten in way over her head this time. Now she was possibly facing a felony. And the police already had more than enough evidence to lock her away for a long time.

All they needed to cinch the case was a confession.

"Lucy didn't do it," he heard himself say, his mind clouded with images of Lucy undergoing arrest and a trial. Sitting in a cold, empty jail cell until all her optimism and exuberance and dreams faded away.

Babette rolled her eyes. "Come on, Chamberlin. You used to be a cop. A real hotshot, from the stories down at the station. We've got previous criminal activity, a statement that points to motive and even the fingernail file she used to pick the lock. If she's not guilty, then who is?"

"Me."

9

EVERYONE IN THE ROOM turned to gape at him. Nick met Lucy's gaze; her big brown eyes reflected a raw emotion that made him swallow hard and look away. His unplanned outburst surprised him almost as much as the rest of them. But he did it for Lucy. And he'd do it again in a heartbeat.

"That doesn't any make sense," Babette said at last.

Nick folded his arms across his chest, hoping his bluff worked well enough to delay an arrest—at least long enough for Lucy to get an alibi, or a good lawyer. "It does if you actually follow through all the leads in the case. You should have learned that your first week at the police academy. Have you even interviewed the *alleged* victim?"

Officer Madison and Babette looked guiltily at each other. "Well...not yet. The victim's mother, Letitia Beaumont, reported the burglary. She was quite upset about it and wanted immediate action. We haven't been able to locate Miss Beaumont."

Nick shook his head. "So you two go off half-cocked and accuse an innocent woman of the crime? That's not exactly proper police conduct."

Babette bristled. "*You* should talk, Chamberlin! You just got out of prison for *improper* conduct."

"That's right," Nick said, keeping his voice relaxed and even, hoping some of Lucy's vivid imagination and storytelling techniques had rubbed off on him. "My prison record is what Vanessa found so appealing about me. We had a date last Friday evening. You can verify it with Jacques at Château Pierre. I'm sure he'll remember me.''

Babette scribbled the name in her notebook.

''That's when Vanessa asked me to play out her little fantasy,'' Nick continued. ''I think she called it The Criminal and the Debutante.''

''I knew that girl was trouble,'' Sadie muttered under her breath.

Nick cleared his throat, more than a little uncomfortable describing a sexual fantasy with his grandmother in the room. Lucy didn't look too happy, either. In fact, his sweet librarian looked downright lethal.

''I was supposed to break into her town house and ransack it until I found her in the bedroom,'' he said, hurrying through the story. ''And then...well, I'm sure you can figure out the rest.''

Officer Madison tugged at his shirt collar. ''Gee whiz.''

''But Vanessa wasn't in the bedroom, or anywhere else in the place,'' Nick said, before Lucy could grab the nearest aerosol can. ''She must have forgotten to mark our date down on her social calendar.''

''So how do you explain the fingernail file we found? The one belonging to Miss Moore?'' Babette asked.

''Easy,'' Nick replied. ''I've been staying at Lucy's place for the last few days, so I've had access to all her things.''

''Then we'll find your fingerprints on it?'' Officer Madison asked.

''I wore gloves and a ski mask,'' Nick explained. ''It was all part of the fantasy.'' He cleared his throat. ''Now you can find Vanessa and verify the story or you can arrest me...or Lucy, and give the cops down at the station a good laugh.''

Officer Madison's freckled cheeks flushed with embarrassment. He turned to Babette. "Maybe I'll go out to the squad car and radio Lieutenant Delaney about the situation."

Babette nodded. "And I'll try phoning Miss Beaumont at her town house again. If she's still not there, I'll call around to see if I can track her down."

"You can use the telephone in the den," Sadie said, leading her from the living room as Officer Madison ducked out the front door.

"The Criminal and the Debutante?" Lucy asked once they were alone.

"I know what you're thinking." He moved closer to her, dropping his voice to a whisper.

"I don't think you do. I could strangle you."

He held up both hands. "Wait a minute. I made up that story about Vanessa and her fantasy."

"I know you made it up," she said. "It was a great story. Very creative. There's no way you could have had a rendezvous with Vanessa this afternoon. I saw you in the library, remember? You were too worried about your grandmother to indulge in any fantasies."

His fingers brushed a honey blond curl off her cheek. "I don't know about that," he said huskily.

"Pay attention, Nick," she warned. "I'm not through with you yet."

He dropped his hand, frowning at the fierce expression on her face. "If you don't believe my story, why do you look like you want to annihilate me?"

She rolled her eyes. "Because, you big, dumb, noble *jerk,* we wouldn't be in this mess if you weren't always trying to protect me! *I* didn't break into Vanessa's town house, either."

As soon as she said the words, Nick knew she was telling him the truth. He also realized he might have overreacted just a little to the police interrogation. Like confessing to a crime he didn't commit. Again.

He closed his eyes. "I don't believe it."

"Believe it," she said, misunderstanding him. "Somebody set me up while I was busy rescuing your grandmother from her kidnapper. Or rather, the kidnapper from your grandmother."

His eyes flew open. "Gram was *kidnapped?*"

"More like 'voluntarily detained.' Look, Nick, I think it's time we compare notes. Someone is trying very hard to distract us from this case, which can only mean one thing. We're getting too close for comfort."

He couldn't agree more. He'd been fighting the urge to wrap her in his arms since she walked through that front door with his grandmother in tow. He'd wanted to kiss Lucy silly when she'd spouted that convoluted story. And now he wanted to haul her over his shoulder and go on the lam before one of them ended up behind bars.

Nick knew at that moment he loved her.

This revelation was unexpected, overwhelming and inconvenient as hell, considering the circumstances. But his heart overflowed with love for Lucy Moore.

She planted her hands on her hips, looking angry and exasperated and simply adorable. "We're in this together. So no more shutting me out of the case, Chamberlin. Let me be an equal partner in this investigation...or else."

He bit back a smile at the fierce gleam in her eye. "Or else what?"

She tipped up her chin. "Or else I'll be forced to do something drastic. I've got peanut butter and I'm not afraid to use it."

He held up both hands. "All right, I surrender. From now on we're together all the way. But before we can figure out who set you up, we need to get rid of Freckles and Babette.''

Sadie hurried into the living room. ''Nicky Chamberlin, I could wring your neck!''

''Get in line,'' Lucy muttered. ''Can you believe he'd confess to something he didn't do?''

Sadie took a deep breath. ''Yes, I can. He did it a year and a half ago. It seems to be turning into a bad habit.''

''He what?'' Lucy exclaimed.

Nick looked in disbelief at his grandmother. ''You knew?''

She shook her head, her lower lip trembling. ''No, not at the time. I was still in shock. Your grandfather was my entire life. I knew something had been troubling him for weeks. Then he suffered those heart attacks and the next few months passed like a nightmare for me. When I woke up, you'd already been convicted and sentenced.''

Lucy stared up at him as if she'd never seen him before. ''You sacrificed your career and your reputation and your freedom for someone else?''

He shrugged. ''It was just something I had to do.''

''I should have known,'' she said huskily. ''You've always been too honest and noble for your own good.''

Nick turned to his grandmother, unnerved by the raw emotion shining in Lucy's eyes.

''Why do you think Grandpa did it?''

She took a deep breath, then set her mouth in a determined line. ''I think neither my husband nor my grandson was guilty of committing the crime. Or any crime, for that matter. And I refuse to sit idly by and watch it happen all over again. So what can I do to help?''

Lucy snapped her fingers. ''I've got it! A way to get rid of the cops.'' She turned to Sadie. ''Do you remember that book the Merry Widows Club read last July? The title was *High Society Sleuths Go to Vegas.*''

Nick groaned. ''I don't think I want to hear this.''

A slow smile dawned on Sadie's lips. ''Yes, I do remember, and I think I know exactly the scene you mean. But will it work?''

Lucy grinned. ''If it worked for Reginald and Penelope Van Whipple, it will work for us.''

THE CLOSET DOOR CLOSED, blanketing Nick and Lucy in total darkness. Nick heard the scrape of a key in the keyhole, then the sound of Sadie's footsteps fading away.

''This is your great idea?'' he asked, disoriented by the blackness surrounding him and the odor of mothballs in the air. ''Locking us in a closet?''

''It worked in the book.'' Lucy's voice floated toward him. ''The mobsters thought they'd gone out the back door and ran after them. That gave the Van Whipples a chance to escape. When Sadie tells the cops we went out the back door to search for Vanessa ourselves, they'll take after us. That should buy us a little time.''

''I just hope it's enough.''

Silence as thick as the darkness descended between them. Clothes hangers jabbed Nick in the back as he moved to find room in the stuffed closet. His foot collided with a bowling ball, and he swallowed his grunt of pain.

''Are you all right?'' she asked.

''I'm fine,'' he said through clenched teeth, trying to ignore the throb in his big toe. ''We need to put the pieces of this case together and come up with a plan.''

''Good idea. You go first.''

''I found a matchbook at the Hanover Building the night we broke in. Vanessa had an identical matchbook. It was from the Beaumonts' anniversary party on April nineteenth."

"The same night as the fire. It makes sense now."

"What makes sense?" he asked.

"Lily Vyne, the eyewitness. With everything going on, I haven't had a chance to tell you. She saw a man leaving the Hanover Building only moments before the fire. He was in a tuxedo."

"Now all we need is a list of all the guests that attended the party. Cole tried to get it from the Beaumonts but came up empty."

He heard her quick intake of breath. "What's wrong?"

"I've got it."

"What?"

"The list. The invitation list. It's on a computer disk at the library. Mrs. Beaumont always uses the library staff as if we're her social secretaries. I guess she thinks it's one of the fringe benefits for serving on the Heritage Library Foundation. I remember typing the list into the computer and fuming because Melvin wasn't invited."

"Lucy, do you know what this means?" he asked, his blood surging with adrenaline. As a cop, he'd always felt this way right before he'd cracked a case. "Between that list and the eyewitness and the matchbook, we should have enough evidence to convince Cole to reopen the investigation. And it would help if we could prove that you weren't anywhere near Vanessa's place this afternoon. Did anyone else see you besides Gram?"

"A little girl on Bale Street," Lucy replied. "And Weasel."

"Weasel? Why the hell were you with Weasel?"

"Not so loud," Lucy whispered. "I'll tell you later. We don't want Babette and Officer Madison to hear us."

"*I* can hardly hear you," he replied. "You sound all muffled."

"All these coats are smothering me," she complained. "And I can't see a thing."

He reached out for Lucy, grabbing a fistful of faux fur instead. "Just move toward the sound of my voice."

He moved his hands around, searching for her among the old coats and dresses and suits. Then he found her. "I've got your shoulder," he said, squeezing it gently to reassure her. Only, the flesh beneath his hand was round and warm and incredibly soft.

"I know it's been a long time for you, but...that's not my shoulder."

"Lucy," he breathed, his hand lingering there for a long moment before skimming down over her ribs to her slender waist. He pulled her close, inhaling the familiar, sweet scent of her skin. Her hair tickled his nose. All his senses came alive in the darkness. Sound...smell...touch... Now he wanted more than anything to taste her.

He drew his hand slowly back up along her body, allowing it to guide him to her mouth. He heard her intake of breath, felt the delicate skin on her throat pebble beneath his fingertips. Then he found her chin, tipping it up, while his fingers caressed her lips.

"Kiss me, Nick," she said in a sultry whisper. "Kiss me like you never want to stop."

He knew he wouldn't want to stop, knew this was the worst possible time to indulge in the fantasies he'd been having ever since the first moment he met her. But he'd delayed living his life long enough. From now on, Nick Chamberlin planned to enjoy every moment and take advantage of every opportunity.

He gently cupped her face between his palms, then lowered his head until his mouth touched her face. He brushed his lips over hers, so lightly that she moaned for more. His tongue traced the seam of her lips until they parted. He deepened the kiss, moving his mouth against hers in a slow, evocative rhythm. His lips made a leisurely journey across her neck, tasting and caressing, awakening every nerve cell in his body.

"Oh...Nick," she murmured, her lips seeking his once more, teasing and tantalizing. He moaned into her mouth as her hands joined in the fray. She touched him with an enthusiastic curiosity that kindled the fire inside him. The darkness heightened all his senses, making each touch, each sound, each taste, an intimate caress.

Nick forgot about everything except the beautiful, sensuous woman in his arms—until the closet door swung open. They reluctantly pulled apart, squinting at the sudden infusion of bright light.

Sadie stood before them. "I got rid of the heat."

Nick looked at Lucy's flushed cheeks, her red lips and the passion glowing in her big brown eyes, wishing he could just carry her upstairs instead of carrying on with this investigation. But the sooner they solved this case, the sooner they could finish what they started in the closet.

"Ready?" he asked.

She nodded. "I'll go to the library and get the list."

"And I'll track down Cole and we'll meet you there. If he's not home, I've got his pager number back at your apartment. I have a feeling when we tell him about Lily Vyne, this case will break wide open."

"What if she still refuses to talk to the police?"

Nick brushed a stray curl off her cheek. "She'll talk to Rafferty. He's always had a way with women."

Lucy arched a blond brow. "What about you, Nick?"

He grinned. "There's only one woman I'm hoping will want to have her way with me."

Sadie cleared her throat. "Time to get moving, you two." She reached up to kiss Nick's cheek. "Good luck. I'll keep the Stroganoff warm until you come back."

LUCY DIDN'T NEED her nail file to break into the Heritage Library. Her key worked perfectly. But she still felt like an intruder as she moved among the rows of bookshelves, her footsteps echoing in the deserted building.

She'd been in the library after closing time several times before, but the silence seemed ominous now, almost eerie. The streetlights outside illuminated the interior of the library just enough for Lucy to make her way around inside without bumping into anything.

The hairs on the back of her neck prickled as she made her way across the main floor. Her instincts told her that she wasn't safe, but her instincts weren't all that reliable. They hadn't told her that Nick wasn't really a criminal, or that Babette wasn't really a prostitute. Or that peanut butter could be dangerous.

So maybe her uneasiness was due to her overactive imagination. Nick trusted her to handle this part of the investigation alone while he tracked down his old partner. They just had to convince Cole Rafferty to reopen the investigation—and soon, if she wanted to keep Melvin from going through with his escape plans.

Tapping sounds drew her attention to the large windowpanes overhead. She stood immobilized as she peered into the darkness, reminding herself of the tall oak trees lining the walk outside the library. Branches hitting the windowpane. No reason to panic. Neither was that loud creaking noise above her. She looked up at the tiled ceiling. Probably just the building settling. All old buildings made unusual noises. Didn't they?

Lucy told herself she didn't have time to figure out the

source of every mysterious creak and clank. It was only a matter of time before the police tracked her down to question her some more about the break-in at Vanessa's town house. Time that she was wasting by jumping at shadows.

She took a deep, fortifying breath before heading into the tiny audiovisual room. The tables inside were crowded with the library's computers, audiotape recorders, overhead projectors, a VCR and two microfilm readers.

She sat down at a computer terminal and booted up. The library network allowed all the computers to access information from one another. The computer screen glowed a bright phosphorescent green, lighting up the area around her. She typed in her password, then accessed Letitia Beaumont's social file, scrolling down the length of text until she finally found it: the invitation list for Harold and Letitia Beaumont's fortieth anniversary party.

Lucy highlighted the list of over two hundred names, flipped on the laser printer, then clicked on the print icon.

The whir of the printer sounded unusually loud in the empty room. But not quite loud enough to cover the sound of the door to the room creaking open.

A shiver tingled down her spine. She held her breath as her instincts screamed at her to run. Maybe they were wrong again. Maybe Nick had arrived early. Or a ghost roamed the library at night. Or her stalker finally wanted to meet her in person.

"Hello, Lucy."

She turned around, breathing a sigh of relief at the sight of a familiar face in the doorway. "Hello, Lieutenant Delaney. You startled me."

"Sorry about that," he said, sauntering inside the room. "Seems you're wanted downtown for questioning. According to Officers Madison and Gryzynski, you're involved in a burglary."

Her heart sank. She just needed a little more time. Her gaze fell to the printer, slowly spitting out the second sheet of paper full of names and addresses. "I know, Lieutenant. Somebody set me up. Nick and Detective Rafferty should be here in about twenty minutes. Then we can get this all straightened out."

"Let me guess," he said, stepping out of the shadows. "This has to do with the case against your brother."

"I think we've got enough evidence to reopen the investigation," Lucy said, her voice quivering with excitement. "An eyewitness came forward."

His eyes widened at that announcement. "No kidding? An eyewitness?"

Lucy nodded. "She came to the library this afternoon and told me she saw a man in a tuxedo leaving the Hanover Building shortly before the fire started."

The lieutenant shook his head in disbelief. "That's incredible."

"We're close to finding the real arsonist, Lieutenant," she said as the last sheet of paper fell onto the printer tray. "Very close."

He took a step toward her. "A little too close, Lucy," he said, pulling his gun out of his shoulder holster and aiming it straight at her.

NICK CREPT THROUGH the bushes beside Lucy's apartment building, intently watching his prey. He almost hadn't seen the stalker in his race toward Lucy's place to retrieve Cole's pager number. But now there was no mistaking the sound of leaves crunching underfoot and the flash of green polyester between the bare twigs.

"Bird-watching, Lester?"

The man crouching under the window of Lucy's apartment emitted a high-pitched scream. He bolted up to make a run for it, but Nick had already hooked his arm around Lester's throat. "Or maybe you're peeping through windows again?"

Lester whimpered. "Please let me go. I didn't do anything wrong."

"Now that's a matter of opinion, Les." Nick released his hold, but stood blocking the only path to the street. Lester was trapped by hydrangea bushes on one side and the three-story brick apartment building on the other.

"I need to go home now," Lester said, his gaze darting frantically around him, searching for an escape route. "Mother's expecting me. She'll...she'll have my milk ready. She makes me warm milk every night. It helps calm my nerves."

Nick stood with his feet planted wide apart, twirling a stray twig in his hands. "Why would you be nervous, Lester? I'm a perfectly nice guy. Of course, the fact that I'm an ex-con sometimes makes people nervous. You know, we tend to be violent. Explode easily. Sometimes lose control." Nick snapped the twig in half.

Lester emitted a tiny squeak. "What do you want from me?"

"I want to know why you've been stalking Lucy."

"I was not stalking her," Lester said, his indignation momentarily overcoming his fear. "I was spying on her. There's a big difference."

"I'd say about three to five years in the state penitentiary."

Lester blanched. "No! It wasn't my fault. He told me to keep on eye on her. That she might be involved in criminal activity." He swallowed, his Adam's apple bobbing in his throat. "He said it was my civic duty. And I also have a responsibility as library director." Lester sniffed. "We can't have riffraff working at the Heritage Library."

"Riffraff?" Nick echoed, taking a step closer.

Lester backed up against the brick wall, his eyes wide. "Not that I think Miss Moore is riffraff, even if her brother is in jail. She's very pleasant, even though she's always trying to change things around the library. In fact, I wasn't even planning on watching her tonight, but I...I..." His voice trailed off.

"You what?"

"Well, she's very pretty, and Mother doesn't let me date much, so watching Lucy has become sort of my new hobby." Lester tugged at his shirt collar. "I just couldn't stay away...even after you told me that you were handling the investigation."

Nick's eyes narrowed. "I've never even talked to you before tonight."

Lester's head bobbed up and down. "Yes, you did. I was there that night at the Château Pierre, hiding behind the potted palm."

"You?" His jaw clenched. "You followed Lucy to the restaurant?"

"I was supposed to keep an eye on her. Report any suspicious activity. But when you warned me to stay away, I figured he'd told you to spy on Lucy, too."

"Who is *he?*"

"That policeman. Lieutenant Delaney," Lester explained. "He gave me the assignment a few weeks ago. Sometimes I'd call her just to see if she was home, and other times I'd come over here and check on her."

Nick sucked in his breath. *Delaney?* Delaney ordered Lester to keep on eye on Lucy? Why? It just didn't make sense. But the gnawing in Nick's gut told him he didn't like it one bit.

He grabbed Lester by the shirt collar, pulling him toward the street. "I'm going after Lucy. I want you to go down to the police station and tell them everything you told me. Got it?''

``I'll have to call Mother first....'' Lester shouted, but Nick didn't hear him as he raced for his car.

10

LUCY SWALLOWED as she stared into the barrel of a really big gun. Trying not to panic, she asked herself what Penelope Van Whipple would do in this situation. Cause a distraction. Come up with a delay tactic. Wait for the author to write her out of this mess.

The books in the library were filled with heroes. She'd read of their chivalrous escapades countless times. If only one of them would jump off the pages and come to her rescue.

Reginald Van Whipple, where are you when I need you?

Lucy had never wished for a happily-ever-after more than she did at this moment. Only, this wasn't fiction. And that gun gleaming in Delaney's hand wasn't make-believe. She'd have to depend on herself.

"I don't understand," she said, her mind racing in a hundred different directions. She didn't want to die. She needed to keep him talking. Ignore the gun. Buy cat food. Tell Nick she loved him.

That would be the first item on her list when she saw him again—*if* she saw him again. She took a deep breath. "Is this some kind of joke?"

Delaney snorted. "I thought you were a joke the first time we met. A harebrained librarian out to catch a criminal. Even with Chamberlin I didn't think you stood a chance of success. I covered my tracks too well." He motioned to the computer with his gun hand. "You can delete that file now and then turn all those machines off."

Lucy turned back to the computer screen, glimpsing the name of Lieutenant Ed Delaney on the invitation list before she reluctantly hit the delete button. Then, with her hands shaking, she methodically flipped buttons on the machines in front of her.

Delaney moved to the printer, sweeping up the papers she'd just printed off. He folded them and tucked them into his suit coat. "I don't suppose you have any books here on how to silence nosy librarians?"

"I'll have to check the card catalog," she said, edging away from him.

He took another step toward her. "Don't bother. I was never much of a reader anyway. I prefer action."

"Is that why you torched the Hanover Building?" Lucy asked, moving so a table full of audiovisual equipment stood between her and Delaney. "And then framed my brother for the crime?"

He shrugged. "I was just doing my job. As the police liaison for the Friends of Westview Association, that is. They pay me extremely well. Sure beats that measly pension I'll get from the police department. All I have to do is take care of any little problems that crop up—like disposing of traffic tickets or unsuitable men dating their precious daughters."

"The Beaumonts paid you to get rid of Melvin?"

Delaney nodded. "Good old Letitia didn't want to know any of the details. She just wanted Mad Dog Moore out of her daughter's life."

Lucy wished she had a can of hair spray handy right now. Industrial strength.

Delaney sighed. "It all went perfectly until you started

digging around in the case. I thought I could keep an eye on you."

"It was you who broke into my apartment."

He shrugged. "That's what you get for planting phony tips in the newspaper. But now it's getting too messy. Madison and Gryzynski have botched up the investigation of the Beaumont break-in so much that I'll never see you convicted and out of the way. So I guess it's up to me to tie up loose ends."

He pulled a length of clothesline cord out of the back pocket of his slacks. "Good thing I brought some rope."

Just what she needed. A killer with a sense of humor. "You won't get away with this."

"Sure I will. Everybody will think *Floyd* did it." Delaney snorted. "Besides, the only man who ever came close to catching me was old Captain Chamberlin. He suspected the Protégé Project was a front from the very start. I even went to the trouble of planting contraband in his car to discredit him. But then he conveniently had a heart attack. Of course, I never could have predicted his grandson would confess to the crime." He laughed, slapping the rope against his knee. "Isn't that a hoot? The old man never let me out of his sight when I was a rookie. Always hounding me. Passing me up for the big promotions. He didn't think I deserved to be a cop. Just because I cut a few corners along the way and roughed up a couple of hookers. Big deal."

Lucy swallowed. Poor Lily. No wonder she didn't want to come forward.

"Next thing I know, he reports that I've got a gambling problem and Internal Affairs is breathing down my neck. So I decided it was time to get even." Delaney chuckled. "Now the old man's dead and his grandson's brought shame on the great Chamberlin name. Talk about poetic justice.''

''You framed Nick,'' she said, adrenaline fueling her anger. ''Then you framed my big brother.'' She threw back her shoulders. ''And now I'm going to make you pay.''

''Oooh, I'm scared,'' he mocked, laughter shaking the big belly hanging over his belt. ''The big bad librarian is going to get me.''

''You should be scared,'' she warned. ''Librarians are very resourceful.'' Then she flipped on the power switch of the overhead projector in front of her, the intense beam aimed directly at his face.

The bright light blinded him. His gun hand faltered as he brought up his other hand to shield his eyes from the glare.

Lucy ran for the door, making a wide arc around Delaney. She heard his muttered curses as she pulled it open, then his footsteps behind her as she headed for the locked front entrance. Grabbing a book off the shelf of new releases, she hurled it through the electronic sensor near the front doors, then ran for the rows of towering bookshelves.

A piercing alarm sounded throughout the building. Lucy leaned against the biography section, gasping for breath. She knew the security alarm rang at the police station after library hours. She also knew it would take them at least fifteen minutes to get here.

''Don't make me shoot you,'' Delaney said, his voice carrying over the stacks. ''I was going to go easy on you. Tie you up. Set fire to the building. You'd die of smoke inhalation before the flames ever got to you.''

Lucy edged around the nonfiction section, listening intently. By the sound of his footsteps, he was checking each row. *Cautiously* checking each row. Score one for the librarian; she'd obviously taught him not to underestimate her.

Unfortunately, the only weapons left in her arsenal were a hairpin and a number two pencil.

"Letitia Beaumont has been itching to build a new library," Delaney said, his voice uncomfortably close. "Maybe they'll even call it the Lucy Moore Memorial Library."

She swallowed the bubble of hysteria in her throat. Was this supposed to tempt her out of hiding?

"This is your last chance, Lucy."

She could see him now through a small gap in the books on the shelf. Only one row away. He crept nearer, the rope in his hands, his gun still tucked inside his holster—which meant he still didn't consider her much of a threat.

Librarians just don't get enough respect.

She braced her hands on the heavy frame of the ten-foot oak bookshelf. He stood directly opposite her now, only the bookshelf between them. His gaze fell on her through the same small gap. Then he smiled.

Lucy pushed with all her might, tipping the shelf far enough for a cascade of books to rain on Delaney. His shouts filled the air as she rounded the bookshelf to make her escape, Delaney right on her heels.

Then she saw Nick standing by the front desk. Her handsome, brave, *unarmed* hero.

"Nick! I love you!" Lucy shouted, barely avoiding the large rolling book cart in front of him. "Run for it!"

Delaney saw Nick, too, skidding to a stop just before he got within swinging distance. He dropped the rope, reaching for his gun.

"There will be no shooting in the library," Nick said, ramming the solid wooden book cart into Delaney's gut. The lieutenant flipped headfirst into the waist-high cart, his gun skidding away harmlessly, and his head hitting the bottom of the cart with a resounding thud. His flailing legs stuck straight up as he struggled to right himself.

Lucy picked up an oversize edition of *Webster's Unabridged Dictionary* off the front desk and flung it on top of his head. The ten-pound version. Delaney stopped moving.

Nick looked down at her handiwork. ''Remind me to look up the word *concussion* whenever I start underestimating librarians.'' He took a closer look at the unconscious man. ''Or maybe the words *fractured skull.*''

''I didn't mean to hurt him that badly,'' Lucy said, frowning down at the still body.

''Forget about him.'' Nick slowly drew her to him, wrapping her in his strong, protective arms. ''Did you mean it, Lucy? Do you really love me?''

She gazed up into his gray eyes, her throat tight with emotion. She'd never seen him look so vulnerable, so full of hope. ''Yes, Nick. I meant it. I love you. Now and forever.''

He hugged her, burying his face in her hair, squeezing her so tightly she couldn't breathe. And she didn't care.

A weak groan emanated from the book cart. Nick turned her away from it, still holding her close to him. She could feel his heartbeat melding with her own.

''Don't worry about Delaney,'' he murmured against her ear. ''He'll live. Let's just hope he doesn't plead amnesia when it's time to take the witness stand.''

''It doesn't matter,'' she said, pulling away just far enough to smile up at him. ''I've already got his confession.''

His brow furrowed. ''What do you mean?''

''When Delaney showed up in the audiovisual room, I punched the record button on a tape recorder. He thought

I was just shutting down the computer." She took a deep breath as Nick's strength and warmth flowed into her, slowly thawing the icy fear inside her. "So I kept him talking. I thought if he killed me, at least I could save Melvin. Someone would hear that tape and know the truth."

"You amaze me," he whispered, pressing his lips to her hair. Then his mouth sojourned along her jaw, lingering at every point along the way.

"And that's not all," she murmured, distracted by his kisses. "Your grandfather didn't do it."

His lips stilled on her neck. He pulled away just far enough to gaze into her eyes. "What did you say?"

"I said your grandfather was innocent. Delaney knew your grandfather was on to him, so he planted the marijuana in his car. Only, you took the blame instead. I've got it all on tape."

"You've got it all on tape?" he repeated, looking completely stunned. *"You got it all on tape?"*

She nodded. "I keep telling everyone librarians are very resourceful. Why won't anyone believe me?"

"I believe you," he declared, lifting her up in his arms and whooping with joy. He twirled her around until she was dizzy, before setting her back on her feet.

"And I love you, Lucy," he said, proving his point by kissing her senseless. "I want to spend the rest of my life with you." He grinned. "And then some."

Lucy melted against him. Dizzy, breathless and happier than she'd ever been in her life. Only a tiny twinge of doubt remained. "I love you, too, Nick," she said. "I think I've loved you since the night of the stakeout. But are you sure? Absolutely sure? I know I've been nothing but trouble for you since the first day we met."

"You are trouble," he agreed, his gray eyes shining with

passion and promise. "Just the kind of trouble I want in my life."

THE WESTVIEW POLICE station buzzed with the news of the veteran officer gone bad. Cole ushered Nick and Lucy into his office to escape the pandemonium.

Cole perched on the corner of his desk. "We're bringing Letitia Beaumont in for questioning, as well as Ralph Rooney and several other members of the Friends of Westview Association. Looks like they had quite a setup."

"What about my brother?" Lucy asked.

"Mad Dog Moore's been notified about the new developments in the case. He'll go before a judge tomorrow morning to have the charges dropped, but that should just be a formality. Then he'll be a free man."

"You did it," Nick said, wrapping his arms around Lucy, and pulling her close. "You saved your brother."

"*We* did it," she replied, snuggling against him. "Proved Melvin innocent. *And* you. Neither one of you is guilty of anything."

"Except loving you." Nick kissed the top of her head. "This is the luckiest day of my life. And believe it or not, it's a Monday." He shook his head in disbelief. "Or maybe the luckiest day of my life is the day we met."

"That was a Monday, too," Lucy reminded him. "And I knew you were the perfect man for the job. The police department was crazy to let you go."

"It just so happens the police captain agrees with you," Cole replied.

"What are you saying?" Nick asked, his arm circling Lucy's waist.

Cole grinned. "Due to the severe shortage of police personnel and the fact that Delaney confessed to framing you a year and a half ago, the captain wants you reinstated on the force. Effective immediately.''

Lucy turned into his arms. ''Oh, Nick! How exciting!''

Cole chuckled. ''Nick may not agree with you.''

Nick forced his attention from a warm and loving Lucy to his old partner. ''Are you kidding? I can't wait to get back to police work.''

''That's great,'' Cole replied. ''Because you've already been given an assignment—a suspected embezzlement scheme. And it's one of those good news, bad news cases.''

''Save the good news for last,'' Lucy said, a rosy blush in her cheeks. ''I like happy endings.''

Cole nodded. ''Okay, the bad news first, then.'' He turned to Nick. ''You're going undercover as one of the employees at Farley's Fish Hut.''

Nick groaned. ''And the good news?''

''You get to wear this really cool cod hat.''

Watch for Cole Rafferty's story in
ANNIE, GET YOUR GROOM
from LOVE & LAUGHTER
in late 1999.

CHRISTMAS Treats

PENNY JORDAN,

DAY LECLAIRE &
LINDSAY ARMSTRONG

bring you the best of Christmas romance in this wonderful holiday collection where friends and family gather to celebrate the holidays and make romantic wishes come true.

Christmas Treats is available in November 1998, at your favorite retail store.

HARLEQUIN®
Makes any time special™

Look us up on-line at: http://www.romance.net **PHCT371**

Take 2 bestselling love stories FREE

Plus get a FREE surprise gift!

Special Limited-Time Offer

Mail to Harlequin Reader Service®

3010 Walden Avenue
P.O. Box 1867
Buffalo, N.Y. 14240-1867

YES! Please send me 2 free Harlequin Love & Laughter™ novels and my free surprise gift. Then send me 4 brand-new novels every other month, which I will receive months before they appear in bookstores. Bill me at the low price of $2.90 each plus 25¢ delivery per book and applicable sales tax if any*. That's the complete price, and a saving of over 10% off the cover prices—quite a bargain! I understand that accepting the books and gift places me under no obligation ever to buy any books. I can always return a shipment and cancel at any time. Even if I never buy another book from Harlequin, the 2 free books and the surprise gift are mine to keep forever.

102 HEN CH7N

Name (PLEASE PRINT)

Address Apt. No.

City State Zip

This offer is limited to one order per household and not valid to present Love & Laughter™ subscribers. *Terms and prices are subject to change without notice. Sales tax applicable in N.Y.

ULL-98 ©1996 Harlequin Enterprises Limited

Steamy, festive and forbidden...

THE AUSTRALIANS

Stories of romance Australian-style, guaranteed to fulfill that sense of adventure!

This December look for

Male for Christmas

by Lynsey Stevens

Tayla Greer was happily single until a gorgeous stranger turned up on her doorstep. Rick McCall was funny, sexy and strictly off-limits. But the racing of her pulse told Tayla that her quiet Christmas was turning into a steamy affair!

The Wonder from Down Under: where spirited women win the hearts of Australia's most independent men!

Available December 1998
at your favorite retail outlet.

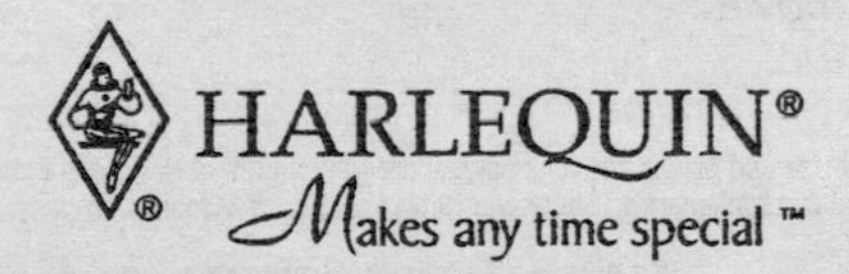

Look us up on-line at: http://www.romance.net **PHAUS6**

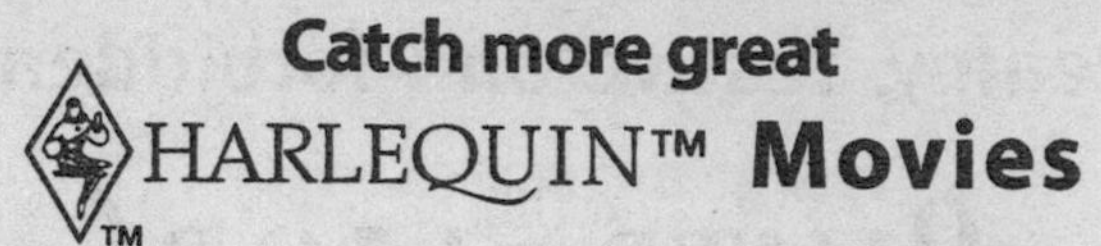

Premiering November 14th

Broken Lullaby

Starring Mel Harris and Rob Stewart.
Based on the novel by bestselling author Laurel Pace

Don't miss next month's movie!
Premiering December 12th
Recipe for Revenge
Based on the novel *Bullets Over Boise* by bestselling author Kristen Gabriel

If you are not currently a subscriber to The Movie Channel, simply call your local cable or satellite provider for more details. Call today, and don't miss out on the romance!

HARLEQUIN®
Makes any time special™

100% pure movies.
100% pure fun.

Harlequin, Joey Device and Makes any time special are trademarks of Harlequin Enterprises Limited. The Movie Channel is a trademark of Showtime Networks, Inc., a Viacom Company.

An Alliance Television Production

PHMBPA1198-R

WHEN THINGS START TO HEAT UP
HIRE A BODYGUARD...

AND THEN IT GETS HOTTER!

There's a bodyguard agency in San Francisco where you can always find a HERO FOR HIRE, and the man of your sexiest fantasies.... Five of your favorite Temptation authors have just been there:

JOANN ROSS ***1-800-HERO***
August 1998
KATE HOFFMANN ***A BODY TO DIE FOR***
September 1998
PATRICIA RYAN ***IN HOT PURSUIT***
October 1998
MARGARET BROWNLEY ***BODY LANGUAGE***
November 1998
RUTH JEAN DALE ***A PRIVATE EYEFUL***
December 1998

HERO FOR HIRE
A blockbuster miniseries.

Available at your favorite retail outlet.

HARLEQUIN® Temptation

Look us up on-line at: http://www.romance.net HTEHFH

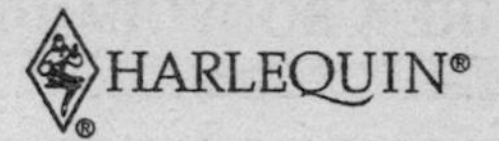

Not The Same Old Story!

Exciting, glamorous romance stories that take readers around the world.

Harlequin Romance®

Sparkling, fresh and tender love stories that bring you pure romance.

HARLEQUIN® *Temptation*

Bold and adventurous—Temptation is strong women, bad boys, great sex!

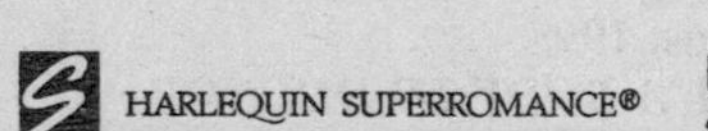

Provocative and realistic stories that celebrate life and love.

Contemporary fairy tales—where anything is possible and where dreams come true.

HARLEQUIN®
INTRIGUE®

Heart-stopping, suspenseful adventures that combine the best of romance and mystery.

LOVE & LAUGHTER™

Humorous and romantic stories that capture the lighter side of love.

Look us up on-line at: http://www.romance.net HGENERIC

The Gifts of Christmas

Join three of your favorite historical romance authors as they celebrate the festive season in their own special style!

Mary Balogh
Merline Lovelace & Suzanne Barclay

bring you a captivating collection of historical romances.

Indulge in the seasonal delights of Regency and medieval England and share in the discovery of unforgettable love with *The Gifts of Christmas.*

Available in November 1998,
at your favorite retail store.

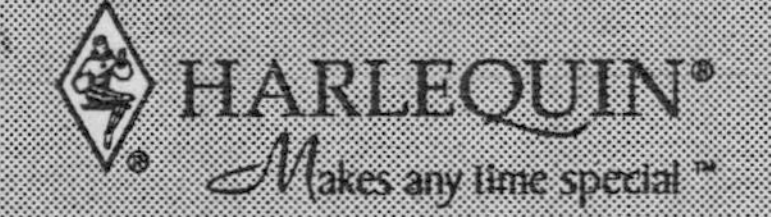

Look us up on-line at: http://www.romance.net

PHGC372

LOVE & LAUGH

INTO DECEMBER!

#57 GIFT-WRAPPED BABY
Renee Roszel
Hallie St. John knew her way around babies, having raised three stepsisters, but finding one under her Christmas tree had her stumped. She discovered that the little pink bundle was meant for her neighbor Nate Hawksmoor, who didn't know a thing about babies. Which left Hallie the impossible task of getting the studly bachelor started on his journey into fatherhood....

#58 NAUGHTY OR NICE?
Stephanie Bond
Eric Quinn Stanton, corporate hatchet man, had never let pleasure interfere with business—until now. Arriving early *and* incognito at the Chandelier House, he planned to see what was working...and what wasn't. Unfortunately, he couldn't see past general manager Cindy Warren's beautiful green eyes...or her other generous assets. But would Cindy still want him when she discovered he was more *naughty* than nice?

Chuckles available now:

#55 THE WEDDING KNIGHT
Jenna McKnight
#56 MONDAY MAN
Kristin Gabriel